I AM RAHAB: A Novel

Part 3

by JC Miller

©Jess, Mo' Books

I AM RAHAB

JC MILLER

Dedicated to Mommy, I miss you.

I AM RAHAB

JC MILLER

Copyright © 2019 J.C. Miller.

All rights reserved. No part of this publication may be reproduced, distributed, or transmitted in any form whatsoever—without the prior written permission of the publisher, except in the case of brief quotations embodied in critical reviews and certain other noncommercial uses permitted by copyright law. For permission requests, write to the publisher at the address below.

ISBN: 978-1-7339386-2-4
Library of Congress Control Number: 2019911966

This is a work of fiction. Any references to historical events, real people, or real places are used fictitiously. Names, characters, and places are products of the author's imagination or used in a fictitious manner.

The Holy Bible, New International Version®, NIV® Copyright © 1973, 1978, 1984, 2011 by Biblica, Inc.™ Used by permission. All rights reserved worldwide.

The World English Bible is in the Public Domain. However, "World English Bible" is a Trademark.
"Aba Daba Honeymoon" written and published by Arthur Fields and Walter Donovan in 1914. Credit: Library of Congress, Music Division.
"Bring me the sunset in a cup" by Emily Dickinson, written in 1924.
"Friend We Have in Jesus" by Joseph M. Scriven, written in 1855 and composed by Charles Crozat Converse in 1868.
Front cover art: Brittany Lewis, Yum Productions Art
Book graphic design: Chanel Smith, WPD Media LLC
Editing: Tiya Marshall, Marshall Editing and Consulting

Printed in the United States of America.

I AM RAHAB

First printing edition 2019.

Jess, Mo' Books LLC
P.O. Bx. 1808
Albrightsville, PA. 18210
JessMoBooksLLC.Wixsite.com/jmbllc

JC MILLER

Table of Contents

Prologue

Section One: Jericho
Lights, Camera, Action,
Man of The House
White Knight
No Whistles Needed
Penthouse Apartment

Section Two: Resurrection
An Unexpected Guest
Bittersweet Aftertaste
When The Streets Call
Invited To Stay
Closure

Section Three: The Land of Milk and Honey
Bonnie And Clyde
Game Changer
Pole Life
The Proposition
Voodoo Doll
The Spies
Lights Out

Section Four: Behind The Wall
Informer
Not A Little Girl
The Last Time
Safe Arms
Columbo
Bayou Boy
Scarlet Covering
C.R.E.A.M

Section Five: The Wall Tumbles Down
A Message
Trumpets
Rise and Go
A Door of Hope
Virtuous Wife
Ghetto Heaven
The Delivery Seventh Round
Hosanna! Hosanna!
The Smell Of Death
By Faith

Epilogue - The Biblical Story Of Rahab
Character Glossary

JC MILLER

PART 3

PROLOGUE

If it is possible to smell death, Rahab can smell it on Jeremy. The foul odor passes through his pores and ripples from his breath.

"Why, Rah? Why?" he shouts over her silent terror. But she can't speak. There's nothing to say; her words can't undo what's already been said. She's his captive, yet she's aware that she's more than a prisoner.

Jeremy's mind screams for him to *surrender, raise the white flag!* But prison isn't an option. *Yo! Players don't go out like that. They go out HARD.* His sanity debates with the sense of insanity gripping him. Rahab's trembling body, held against his, alerts him; *it's not about the game anymore. She's involved.* He releases a sigh of despair.

"I love you," he reluctantly confesses; three words he's never uttered before. He then plants a sloppy wet kiss on her forehead. "If this is it...it's gonna be you and me forever, *Bonnie* and *Clyde* style," he concludes, drawing Rahab closer as though trying to consume her. His trembling hand tightly grips the gun he is pressing against her temple.

Click. Jeremy cocks the pistol, ignoring the pleas from those in the room. All he can hear is his own heavy breathing. *I always hated the way that movie ends.* Remembering Bonnie and Clyde were killed in cold blood, Jeremy prefers to hold his and Rahab's destinies in his hands.

At that moment, time stands still. Rahab's family, helplessly watching the ordeal, freeze. Their stone-like faces grimace in agony. Rahab's tears stop flowing and become plastered to her face. She can't move; her body is stiff. From the corner of her eye, she looks up at Jeremy. His eyes, frozen upon her, have lost their intensity. He doesn't look like himself, and he seems conflicted, an inner war plays on his long face. Rahab's body becomes numb as a calming peace washes over her. She closes her eyes and gives everything she has to Him, the Lord.

BANG! The gun fires.

The room falls silent. All that Rahab can hear, is the pounding of her heart from the inside of her chest. She can see herself falling in slow motion backward into a large dark hole. From her mind's eye, she can see the orange glow of Jeremy's cigar and him sitting in a red leather Queen Anne high-back. "I'm your white knight...the black Jesus," he proclaims then laughs heartily but no sound comes from his mouth. *Am I dead?*

Her life vividly flashes before her.

JERICHO

JC MILLER

LIGHTS, CAMERA, ACTION,

From the darkness of a full room, Rahab bravely awaits her cue to start dancing. Her feet, planted firmly in the middle of a small circular black lacquer stage, itch to run the other way. But Puah's words come to mind.

"Les haricots ne sont pas salés," Rahab whispers to herself. "The snap beans need salt," she repeats.

An illuminating, blue-hued spotlight beams down. Excitement fills the air. Under the cast lighting, Rahab stands assertively. What appears as confidence is her determination to save her family from poverty. They have lived in the welfare hotel for a year too long.

The electric guitar intro to *"Kiss"* by *Prince* ripples through the smoky room. Rahab deeply exhales and closes her eyes, taking her mind back to dancing at the loft and Jayson's smiling eyes gazing at her from the DJ booth.

"Take it off!" A stray voice comments, louder than the other chants coming from the sea of unknown faces wide-eyed in tormenting lust.

Rahab opens her eyes, knowing she needs to give them what they came for. She quickly places the chained medallion around her neck between her ample bosom and quivers her entire body, starting at her feet and moving all the way up, causing an eruption of whooping.

Wearing a lace crop top and tight matching spandex bell-bottoms, she mesmerizes the audience of clamoring men. The replicated *"Kiss"* video outfit she's wearing is an original creation by her best friend, Lydia, who turned out to be quite the seamstress. All of Rahab's outfits are custom made, one-of-a-kind, and attracting purchasing interest from other dancers. Little do they know Lydia barters for her material from flea markets, thrift shops, and budget-friendly fabric stores.

Adorned in hues of purple, Lydia's favorite color, Rahab captivates the crowd. The scent of the lavender and rosemary oils that she massaged into her skin drifts through the room with each alluring movement. Like the dancer in the *Prince* video, Rahab's hair, now dyed black, is slicked back into a ponytail. A long black sheer veil, shimmering with mica flakes, hides her face. She teasingly uses it to cover the heads of men waving large bills. The New Orleans raised Creole beauty allows them only a glimpse of her curvaceous body. She's the queen of the bayou, *Voodoo Doll*. The bewitching but not overbearing aroma of her body oil flows through the veil, warranting the allotted men's sweet dreams of her later. Her Big Mama used to say, "One day you gon' be glad you know bout dis here o'l. Not only does it keeps de bugs off ya, it keeps ya skin young and de smell drives men crazy for true."

Rahab collects their money and provokes them into frenzies with seductive gestures and discarded garments, then winks and blows red-lipstick kisses. Her sets aren't raunchy like the other girls. Her seductive presence and ability to manipulate through dance make up for distasteful tricks.

Silas stands close by, watching the crowd and protecting his sister. At seventeen, he's 6'4" and has the same build his father used to work hard on. Spending a year in juvenile detention does a body with nothing to do but lift weights *good*.

JC MILLER

MAN OF THE HOUSE

Silas was the last to crumble after his grandfather, Richard's death. His pain was subtle. He held it. Instead of mourning for the loss, he aimed to replace him. He had to become the man of the house, especially after finding out that Lydia was pregnant with his baby.

Lydia proved to be the type of female who would always have Silas' back. The night of Richard's death, she jumped into action and helped him and Rahab defend themselves against their grandmother, Mags, who was consumed with sorrow, fear, and anger. So, when Lydia finally confessed her pregnancy and fear of her stepfather, who was now back home, Silas, along with a group of his friends, didn't think twice about setting out to her mother's apartment and giving the stepfather a good old-fashioned *beatdown*.

"You let this douchebag beat up on ya daughter?" Silas yelled, questioning Lydia's mother as she assisted her badly beaten partner. She didn't respond. She only cried hysterically. "Le-Le and our baby will be living with me. Comprende?" He boldly announced, taking Lydia's hand like a king proclaiming his throne. Her mother started to oppose it, but she was ashamed. She knew her daughter was bait in their household and she couldn't muster the strength to leave her man and start over.

Silas' family needed him, so he stepped up his narcotic sales game. He ran the streets with a purpose other than mischief in mind, doing all the wrong things for all the right reasons. When he came out of *juvie*, he briefly escorted his stepfather, Mr. Jenkins, on his *Three Card Monte* hustle, but Silas wasn't impressed. He wanted to help the family, but he wasn't accustomed to making pennies. *Three Card Monte* wasn't worth breaking the mandates of his probation. He quickly gave in to Rahab's pleading of needing a manager to book her in strip clubs. He didn't fancy the idea, but she had tried doing it herself and was nearly raped. Silas could book Rahab's jobs, protect her from foul play, get his *GED,* and keep his probation officer off of his back all at the same time. He was a swindler by nature. Making money with Rahab was easier than conning the streets.

    Rahab had recently graduated high school and was ready to pursue her dream of becoming a full-time professional dancer on Broadway. At first, she took the auditioning route and had some callbacks but quickly discovered *you're nothing without a manager.* A beautiful face gets you noticed as far as the casting couch. Every hiring had a stipulation that required her to *lay on her back.* When she rejected their offers, they rejected her. Rahab desperately wanted to make money but being paid for sex wasn't at the top of her list. Her family needed a home and Mags was rotting away in Creedville Psychiatric Center, a hospital for the insane. So, Rahab convinced herself to use her talent and looks to make *fast money.*

    Instead of the *hood holes* that Rahab previously danced in Silas took her downtown to the privately-owned gentlemen's clubs. Initially, they were turned down because of her age and alcohol laws. But Rahab quickly learned to dance first and answer questions later. On their next outing, the first club owner that saw her immediately loved her. When he discovered she was seventeen, he decided to overlook the minor detail if she worked off the books and carried a fake ID.

The work wasn't easy. They encountered every type of sleaze from all walks of life. In the beginning, Silas literally fought for their livelihood. He quickly caught on to the hustle and learned that everyone had a hand out for money. Everyone from the DJ to door security had to be paid in order for their nights to run smoothly. To make up for the lost money, Silas started negotiating private dances after Rahab's sets. Most clubs have a no-touch policy but don't always enforce it, so Rahab dances with Silas a blow of a whistle away.

On a good night, they pull in anywhere between four and five hundred dollars. The family is able to afford to leave the welfare hotel they live in, but the only adult with actual legal proof of income is Mr. Jenkins. His income doesn't meet the requirements for apartments they want, and it's too much for the public assistance they need.

As of recent, Rahab's been working hard on a plan to obtain a dwelling they'd be proud to call home. She aspires to move the family into an affordable duplex in Co-op City. She figures with the amount of money she makes, even after paying Silas, and the cost of a hassle-free work environment, she can save to buy one and use Mr. Jenkins' credentials.

I AM RAHAB

WHITE KNIGHT

The land, through which we have gone to spy it out, is a land that eats up its inhabitants; and all the people who we saw in it are men of great stature.
Numbers 13:32

  Rahab boldly enters a private room, brashly lit in flashing red lights. She turns on "Between the Sheets" by *The Isley Brothers*, her *go-to* dance track. It's something about the soulful arrangement that stimulates her into provocative dance. Her movements *make love* to the quiet storm/funk fusion song even when she doesn't feel like dancing. This particular evening is one of those nights she can use the extra motivation. It's her eighteenth birthday, and she'd rather be home.
  Rahab strides toward the pole in the middle of the small mirrored room as though on a fashion runway, repeating to herself, *"the snap beans need salt."* The man, patiently watching from a red, leather, *Queen Anne* high-back wing chair, drags on a cigar. One leg is crossed over the other in an open crotch position. Rahab, still wearing the shimmering black sheer veil, grabs the pole and rolls her eyes. *Open crotch men* usually give her a hard time. A balloon snifter glass, partially filled with an amber-colored liquor, is cupped in his right hand with the short stem passing through his fingers. The man holds up his left pointer finger and motions her over before the music can fully inspire her. Rahab rolls her eyes again. *This guy is going to be a real jerk.* She makes sure her whistle is around her neck.

"There's a no-touch policy, sir," she states over the music. She sashays toward him, tugging at her two-piece eggplant-colored sequined bathing suit. Most men come ready to negotiate offers for her to sleep with them. Some offers are tempting, but Rahab hasn't been with anyone in that way since Jayson.

She throws the glistening black veil she's wearing over his head, not sure if he wants a close-up or a conversation. *Wow, he's dark as night.* She begins a lap dance. All she can see is the white of his eyes and the orange glow of the cigar held in his mouth. He rudely puffs and blows smoke rings in her face. She coyly smiles and lightly blows at the smoke.

"Turn the music off," he states as though not moved by her suggestive teasing.

"What?"

"Can you turn the music off?" he repeats, enunciating every word as though she's hard of hearing or mentally challenged.

Rahab sucks her teeth and sighs. *I wonder how much he paid? I doubt enough to be working my nerves.* She parades to the stereo, caring less now if she appears *sexy* and turns the CD off. The mysterious gentleman chuckles inwardly as he observes her stride. Her playful innocence intrigues him. She swishes around with one hand on her hip, facing the stranger and awaiting further instructions.

"Now, that's better. Don't you think? Now, all we need is to do something about these dreadful red lights," he states in a deep almost scary voice. *Darth Vaderish.*

Rahab clicks a switch, illuminating the room. Then shuts the red lighting off. A handsome, well-dressed, smooth, dark brother sits in the leather high-back chair looking like a king.

Hmph, what's this cutie doing here?

The ritzy private club is often patronized by refined Caucasian men sneaking away from their wives for an evening of lust. Rahab is accustomed to them and spoiled bachelors living it up on daddy's dollar. Then, there's the usual perverts and techy geeks paying to see naked women rather than taking the chance to get to know someone. This mysterious man meets none of the standard profiles.

He'd fit in better at the Player's Club uptown.

He clenches his cigar between his white teeth and gestures her over.

"I can't dance without music, sir," Rahab advises, walking back toward the handsome man trying not to seem intrigued by him. She is. She tosses the veil from over her face, needing a closer look.

Oh yeah, he's fine.

"I don't want no cheap lap dance, I want you," he declares, placing his cigar in a nearby ashtray.

He's been scouting the Creole beauty for three weeks. He overheard a few visitors at his club in Harlem raving about *Voodoo Doll* and decided to see for himself.

"I'm no prostitute," Rahab clears up, stopping in front of him. Her stance is powerful and confident. Her hands are on her hips, and her feet are planted firmly ajar. *I don't care how fine he is.* She is impressed with his immaculate *S-Curl* parted box fade.

"I don't pay for sex," he clarifies, smirking then sipping his warm *XO Cognac*. He doesn't remove his eyes from her.

"What is it that you want, a therapist, an escort…mommy? My time is money," she informs rolling her neck, Puah style.

The man smiles revealing perfect teeth. *Yes. I gotta have her.* "My time is money as well, Miss Voodoo Doll. And, I can't say that I'm wasting it right now. This is an investment. The beginning stages of something…sweet."

He uncrosses his leg and crouches over, resting his forearms on his knees. He examines Rahab from her thrift shop-purchased, brand-named stilettos to the crown of her head. He's done his homework and knows her story.

Noticing his scrutiny, Rahab straightens her shoulders so as not to fold under warped judgment. "I'm paid well here. So, no, I'm not interested in your business. I have plans of my own I'm saving for," she relates, defending herself and her shoes. She's also used to club owners trying to buy her out. It's not the private club's money that holds her dedication. She finally feels safe and doesn't want to start the familiarity process over.

"Oh, I can tell you're a businesswoman," he confirms, reaching out to grab her thighs. They look toned, yet soft and feminine. He pauses, holding his hands up in an *I surrender* position. "Mother, may I?" he teases.

Rahab doesn't answer. She twists her lips and shifts her hip to the side.

"You see Miss…Rahab Auguste, I want you. As a matter-of-fact, you're already mine." He glides his fingertips up her legs after making the confident announcement as though an old lover.

Okay, this brother's crazy. She starts to blow her whistle, having had enough of him. The man begins to laugh. Haunting laughter.

"Is that for your brother? Sorry, I mean manager," he teases, pointing at the whistle and laughing heartily. "If it is, Silas is enjoying drinks with his new partners. He knows a good deal when he hears one." He leans back and crosses his leg.

"My brother and I work together," Rahab states, ready to leave and check on Silas.

"Well, that's *ONE* reason I'm here. Your brother wants what's best for you and your family. I have a business proposition that will benefit everyone. A beautiful girl like you deserves more than hand-me-downs and restless nights in a welfare hotel," he airs, reminding her of her shoes and situation.

Her face flushes, and she turns away, not wanting the bold stranger to see her surprise and embarrassment.

Why would Silas tell him all of that? It's none of his business.

"Allow me to explain in a more...desirable setting." The man is now standing and lightly cupping her shoulders. She can feel his body heat, and he smells as good as he looks.

Her scent is driving him mad. Every ounce of his body desires her, but he wants more than a one-night stand. He's a hustler. A gambling man. Rahab is a royal flush. "The *second reason* I'm here is that I hear it's your birthday." Now he's rubbing her arms with his warm hands. He moves in closer. "Let's celebrate together. This time tomorrow, you and your family will be in your new home."

Rahab quickly turns in interest. *Is he legit?* She gives him the once over. *Silas wouldn't abandon me otherwise.*

The man steps back, smirking. With his hands placed behind his back, he slowly spins like a runway model. Pleased with him, Rahab rationalizes his birthday offer.

"You're cocky, aren't you?" she assumes, seductively smiling. She rolls her shoulders and sticks out her bosom, falling back into her *Voodoo Doll* persona.

"I know what I want," he answers, confident that she finds him pleasing.

"What's your name? Being that you know everything about me."

He moves in even closer. Towering over her, he takes Rahab into his arms and whispers in a low sultry voice. "I'm that white knight. The Black Jesus, Jeremy Cole. Those I call friends, call me Jeri. Make sure that's what *you* call me."

Rahab wraps her arms around his neck. She's aware that he can be a *white knight* to them, but she's leery of *the cost?*

"Where you taking me for my berf'day, Jeri?" she questions in her new sharp uptown accent.

"That's for me to know, and for you to enjoy; just remember one thing..." he declares, slightly swaying her.

"What?" *Here we go.* She twists her mouth, expecting the million-dollar answer. Sex.

"You owe me a dance. That *Isley Brothers* joint is *fresh.*"

I AM RAHAB

NO WHISTLES NEEDED

When Rahab stepped into the back of Jeremy's limousine, she had no expectations for the evening, other than having a good time and finding out the truth about Jeremy. She hadn't imagined, over chocolate-covered strawberries and sparkling champagne, how swiftly her life would change.

She studied Silas along with the two other guys riding with them in the limo. Silas was fidgety. He wrung his wrists and blew into clenched hands. Jeremy's proposal seemed perfect to him, a little too perfect, and that made him nervous. Silas caught Rahab's gaze and shyly smiled and winked at her. The opportunity for them to speak in private hadn't arisen. He knew she had questions and doubts. She did, but based on Jeremy's first impression, she was willing to hear him out.

Taking notice of Silas' anxiety, Rahab's instinct to lead and protect him kicked in. She decided she would personally deal with Jeremy Cole. *It can't be that bad. After all, we are in his limo, and man-o-Manischewitz is he fine.* Everything about Jeremy screamed caution, yet he was as tempting as a *SEE*-food dinner after a fast.

Rahab gathered her slightly damp hair over one shoulder, releasing the fresh scent of oils, and adjusted her form-fitting plum-colored dress. She crossed her legs and leaned against Jeremy, forcing him to throw an arm around her shoulders. Content with his reaction, she wrapped her arms around his waist and made herself comfortable as he continued to drink and joke with the fellas. She wanted him to know that she was ready to play with the *big boys*. Jeremy bit down on his bottom lip. He nodded his head in agreement; he knew exactly what she was saying.

Jeremy wined and dined Rahab as promised, pulling out all the stops. They ate at *Sweetwater's* while listening to live music. Since she was from Louisiana, Jeremy knew she would appreciate their Cajun shrimp gumbo. She did. After dinner, they hit *Bentley's* for dancing. The guys, along with a few eager females, sat in the VIP section *poppin' bottles* of champagne while Rahab *revamped her life* on the dance floor. It had been a while since she danced solely for self and the DJ played all of her favorite songs. Jeremy watched intensely from VIP. She was indeed intriguing.

By closing, the DJ announced, "This one's for the ladies and a special birthday girl in particular." Rahab spun around, attempting to locate the voice. "So, homies hold that cutie real tight. You might just get lucky tonight. If you do, you can thank me later. Because Jay-Skii Money is *Audi 5000*! I just dropped the bomb on this mutha tonight. Peace."

Jayson and Silas stood behind the DJ booth smiling as "Very Special" played. Jayson pressed two fingers against his mouth and blew a kiss toward Rahab. She gasped and beamed brightly, swaying to the old love song. Remembering her necklace, she pulled the hanging medallion from underneath her dress and dangled it for Jayson to see. Holding back tears, she tossed him back a kiss. Jeremy appeared out of nowhere with a birthday cake full of sparkling candles. Rahab couldn't help but cry. The evening was perfect. It'd been a long time since she felt special. Jeremy passed the cake to his partner and held her in his arms. They blew out the candles together. Everyone in the club clapped, and the dream was over.

Jeremy's partners took cabs their separate ways. Hesitant to leave, Silas hugged and kissed his sister, questioning if she wanted him to hang around.

"I'll be fine." She'd taken a liking toward Jeremy. "Don't wait up!" she yelled as Silas walked away with his head hung low. Something wasn't settling right.

"I'll get her home safely, bodyguard. No whistles needed," Jeremy teased, laughing.

JC MILLER

PENTHOUSE APARTMENT

Jeremy owns a beautiful condominium building in the Bronx. The penthouse floor is exclusively his, a unique key is needed to access it from the elevator. Four other apartments complete the level, but he failed to mention their use during his bragging. His red, white, gray, and black leather decorated apartment extends from the west side of the building to the east corridor. As he and Rahab tour the four-bedroom penthouse, Jeremy boasts about owning a few other smaller properties in Brooklyn.

"Hold up!" He stops her mid-tour. "Give me a sec."

He removes his linen shirt over his head, revealing a fit, dark chocolate dipped physique. Rahab sighs as he glides down the hall. In her mind, she can hear the beat to *Bob Marley's* "Get Up, Stand Up" accompanying the swag in his *diddy-bop*.

The snap beans could, very well, never need salting again if I handle this right.

Jeremy enters the living room and lies back on a suede, zebra print chaise lounge. With a CD player remote in hand, he turns on the *Isley Brothers'* "Between the Sheets."

"Ayyy!" they shout simultaneously, bopping their heads.

Rahab knows she's up. She sets her purse on a console in the hall and sways her way into the living room. As she approaches, she notices a pole in the corner he's facing.

"Ayyy," they repeat, pointing at it.

With one hand, she effortlessly removes her snug-fitting dress, revealing a coordinating plum bra and panty ensemble. She then tosses the dress to Jeri as she struts by. It was like a magic trick, and that alone impresses him. Lydia's creations are designed for quick removal using a technique she came up with herself. No velcro required. Jeremy confusingly studies the material but not for long. Rahab takes hold of the strategically placed pole and skillfully swings around it. The chords of the bass guitar fill the room, and she drifts away on its beat. She teases and lures Jeremy from his reclined position. Her artistry is beguiling. *Seductive yet tasteful.* He struggles to quiet his longing for her as he shifts to the edge of his seat. He's business first, and *this is* a private audition. When the music stops, Rahab finds herself arched atop his coffee table. Jeremy can't help but clap.

"Dang! Why aren't you in videos, movies, something like that?" he questions, lowering the volume of the next track. "My real question is...can you teach other girls?"

"Yeah, I guess," Rahab answers, wondering what other girls have to do with her.

Jeremy stands and begins to pace the floor.

"Okay, these are my thoughts." He stops in front of her and kneels. "Strip clubs are about sex, we all know that, but it's also an experience. A fantasy. Being close..." He draws in nearer. "...to something you want, but can you have it?" Rahab says nothing. She doesn't know if he's schooling her or propositioning her. "That's what I like about you. You're every man's fantasy, and you don't even know it." He runs his hand up her thigh. Her heart races. "What you do when you dance is emit the spirit that moves you. You captivate. You're like angel dust. You invite people in and, not only will they come back, they're hooked. It's not all about sex; it's all about you." He stands. "Alas, there's only one you. Why should there be *a top act* when every act can be just as good? I want people from all over at my spots spending beaucoup bucks. I want hot girls, the chicks you see in videos, porns, on Broadway. Real entertainers. I don't want no cornball, ashy kneed, cheap thrill," he states, pacing again. "Then, I want these video vixens to double as tricks, escorts, champagne room girls. All that. Make a dream come true. I want dope music, drinks, fly costumes." He stops in front of her and stoops down inhaling. "And that smell. What is that sexy scent? Man! Yuh nuh kno."

Rahab smiles; she knows, but she wonders how it's going to help her family. "It's a family secret...I make it myself."

"Word? That shiznic is off the hook." Jeremy pauses and gazes into her eyes. *She's hot.* He starts to kiss her perfectly pouted lips, but his analytical mind moves faster than his intentions. *Her eyes are beautiful.* "Are those contacts?"

"No!" Rahab laughs. "Er'rything I got is real, boo-boo," she adds, rolling her neck and grabbing her chest.

"Yeah? Let's examine."

Jeremy scoops her up from the table. Her pulse races. She isn't sure she can perform beyond a lap dance. She isn't sure if she wants to. He carries her into a bedroom and flings her on a waterbed. Rahab giggles in fear and surprise. He proceeds to remove the remainder of his clothing. As she poorly attempts not to stare, a knot lodged in her throat. In the past year, she's seen more than enough naked women but never purposely gazed upon a naked man.

Jeremy swaggers slowly toward her and notices she isn't as alluring as when she dances. "You can't possibly be inexperienced?" he teases and laughs off the concept.

Rahab blushes, feeling both embarrassed and terrified.

"You are?" he asks, taken aback.

"No. I'm not. It's just...it's been a while," she shyly holds her head low.

"Aww, how long?" he questions, lifting her chin. Interrogating is an innate behavior of his.

"About...four years," she whispers, hoping he'll find pity and decide to take things slow.

"What? You were like...fourteen. Dang, gyal, yuh still a vir-jan," he voices in a *Jamerican* accent. "Instead of *knockin' boots,* you were knockin' booties. Poppin' *Similac*," he jokes.

"Ha-ha, funny. Thanks for the encouragement. I think I'm ready to leave now." She turns her head and swipes his hand away from her face.

He cups her chin and forces her to look back at him, then stares into her eyes. She imagines the inquisitive thoughts spinning through his genius mind.

"I wanna teach you everything I know...and I'm not talking about sex. I believe that *together* we can rule this game." He pulls her close. "I've been pondering over an idea for a while, and I need a *Bonnie* to my *Clyde.*" Rahab looks perplexed. "You know, a female replica. More than a boo. I know that's you and that turns me on. A *ride or die* partner."

"Business partner?"

"Yeah? But don't get me wrong, I want you. I ain't even gon lie, you mad flyy. But for me, fine chicks are a dime a dozen. With you, I'm turned on by your worth. You're special."

She smiles wide at his compliments, all the while trying to read past his poker face.

"Don't be scared. You can trust me *if* I can trust you. Let's draw from one another."

"Exactly what will I be doing?"

"I want you for myself," Jeremy declares boldly, gently laying her back. "I don't want you dancing in strip clubs anymore. You're a boss, unique like me. Ya stuff ain't for everybody."

Rahab's heart flutters as he acquaints himself with her body. "Tomorrow, I want you and your family to move into this building."

Startled, she starts to sit up, but Jeremy presses her gently back down. "Shhh, listen. Don't talk. Be an observer. Take notes, chile; school is in session." He smirks. "I need a new superintendent for this building. I believe your stepfather can handle that. Of course, he'll have help when needed. I need new security for my spot in Brooklyn. Silas can handle that. He mentioned he wants to stay clean, out of jail, and away from the dope game. I can respect that."

Jeremy had Rahab's full attention. He knew her family was her world. Everything she did, she did for them. She no longer felt afraid. She hardly noticed that he removed her purple ensemble.

"I have a lot of plans for you, but for right now, I need someone to look after some girls. Teach them how to dance. Show them some refinement. Polish them up," he continues, examining every inch of her body as though a doctor. She feels slightly uneasy under his scrutiny.

He notices everything yet finds no faults in her. "I have a fully furnished three-bedroom apartment in the basement and three small studios. The superintendent and his family can live in the apartment. My girls stay in the studios. I like to keep watch over my flock. Do you think you can handle this?" Jeremy finally asks.

The plans become somewhat clear to Rahab, and she's willing to give the opportunity a shot. *No more welfare hotels, a condo?* There is one question: *is he a drug dealer?* She's afraid to ask but also doesn't want anything to do with drugs. Instead of mulling over the matter, she decides to *flip the script* and give Jeremy everything he thinks she doesn't know. She lifts her body from under his roaming hands and turns the music on inside her mind. Blocking out images, smells, and sounds that haunt her, she puts on a show.

Jeremy didn't know everything. He didn't know Rahab's story. She's seen it all and gave all she had to him. She cried after he collapsed fast asleep atop her, but it didn't matter. She had a job to do, and she wasn't afraid anymore.

JC MILLER

RESURRECTION

AN UNEXPECTED GUEST

Time bluntly robbed them of familiarity. Puah fantasized over his return. She believed she was prepared to cast caution to the wind at the chance to be with him again; but gazing upon his diminished body, she realizes her longing was in vain. She never considered the hand that life dealt him.

Minton sort of appeared as randomly as he disappeared; all of a sudden, and unexpectedly, he drifted back into their lives. There was no notice of intent nor warning. Mr. Jenkins inadvertently discovered him while working a street vending gig in Harlem. He saw a man slumped in a wheelchair near a brick wall across from his display table. An adorable child played nearby. She was careful not to wander too far from his presence. Every so often, she stopped playing to sit in his lap and rests her head against his insufficient chest. He would acknowledge her briefly with a slight smile and a pat on the head. Then, she wandered off to play again. She skipped in a circle around his chair, singing and laughing to herself.

Minton assumed Mags and Richard still owned the bar and club in Harlem. He traveled from Brooklyn in hopes of a reunion. Upon hearing the despairing news about his family, Minton made it as far as 125th Street before physically and mentally shutting down. He sat in his wheelchair dazed and out of options. It took every ounce of strength and determination to travel to Harlem that morning. He didn't know if he could conjure up the willpower to make the trip back. Besides, there was no *back* to go to. He left what little he and his little girl owned in hopes that his family would assist them. Minton lowered his head and did what he knew to do; he prayed.

"Father God, I know I'm more than a wretch undone. I'm undeserving of the mercy and kindness You so freely offer," he openly prayed, crying. "Forgive me for my sins. Remove them, as far as the east is from the west. Bury them, please, Lord, in the deepest ocean. Hide me under the cross and see more of You and less of me. Hear my prayers; not for my sake, but for my daughter's. Raise her beyond my imperfections. Spare her the stain of my sins. The foul odor of my filthy rags. Thank You for her. Thank You for caring for her. If it weren't for her life, I would've never given mine to You. Your ways are always perfect. I trust You and You alone. Please guide and keep her safe. Place her with a family that will love her as I do. It's in Jesus' name I pray. Amen."

Minton prayed throughout the day appearing agonized and sorrowful to observers. He wasn't. He was expecting the God he served to provide, and he wasn't moving until something miraculous happened. That or God restored his strength enough to get back to Brooklyn. The longer he sat and prayed the more money passers-by dropped into his lap. His godawful appearance unintentionally granted him pity charity. Minton marveled at the increasing currency and grimaced in confusion and embarrassment. If he had the strength, he would've moved from the busy corner. *God, you surely have a sense of humor.* Minton hoped He had a plan to go along with His jokes. Then, Mr. Jenkins rolled over.

***

I AM RAHAB

"I...I...I know where Minton is!" Mr. Jenkins stuttered as he rolled into the living room.

Puah, Lydia, and Rahab had just settled for dinner in front of the television. The girls planned on spending the evening with Puah. Her newest form of entertainment and distraction was the *boob tube.*

"What!" they responded in amazement, allowing Mr. Jenkins opposed to *Martin* their full attention.

Mr. Jenkins exhaled and slowly continued. "For the first part of the day, this guy kinda looks familiar, but I'm busy trying to sell my hats. I assume he's trying to get in on my corner and I'm pissed. By mid-day, I figure out who he looks like, and I'm wondering if it's him, but he has this little girl, and that's throwing me off. He's also skinnier, much darker, and older than the pictures." Puah's heart sank, and her eyes began to fill up with tears. "Before I leave for the day, I decide to go over and ask for Si and Go-Go's sake." Inwardly, he knew it was for his wife's sake as well. "I say, hey, buddy, you look like someone I sorta know, and he answers... does he owe you money? We both kinda laugh," Mr. Jenkins added, torturing his listeners. He has a way of extending stories. Puah's lips started to quiver. She remembered Minton using the corny punchline whenever anyone would mistake his identity. "So, as it turns out he's on my corner, which is near where *Swamp Water* used to be, looking for you guys. I—"

A pitchy hollow scream interrupted his story. Puah finally broke down. She grasped her seized up chest, as though having a heart attack. "Where is he, James? Where is Senior?"

Mr. Jenkins attempted to resume his story, but he stuttered badly in his eagerness to relieve her tension.

"He's right here." A weak serene voice uttered from the darkness of the hallway. Minton wheeled himself into the living room. Following alongside him was his excited daughter, Charlotte, affectionately named after the street where he left his beloved family.

"SURPRISE!" The tiny child with intellectual disabilities screamed against the family's shock.

The room fell silent. Time froze. Lydia clumsily grasped Rahab's hand. The absence of time didn't allow the chance to heal all wounds. Rahab still carried the burden of her ill-treated past upon her shoulders. She subconsciously rejects male affection and subdues any physical feelings or inner passions that lust, love, or trusting them provides. Intimacy usually ends with her privately crying.

Rahab trembled and squeezed Lydia's hand. Suddenly, she felt like the helpless girl in the back of the van. *Why is he here?* Her buried secrets didn't need resurfacing. She battled the urge to spit in Minton's face.

"I'm sorry you all have to see me like this, but I sure am glad to set these tired eyes on y'all beautiful faces again." A beaming smile widened Minton's narrow face. Some teeth were missing and sunk his cheeks inward. He was no longer clean-shaven and smoothly bald. His patchy hair was thin and gray. His skeletal body, wrapped in oversized layers of neatly pressed clothing, slumped to one side of his wheelchair.

The women wondered how Mr. Jenkins identified him. They were certain they wouldn't have been able. If Minton hadn't appeared as another hustler trying to squeeze in on his turf, Mr. Jenkins probably would have never noticed him. But God.

"Senior?" Puah questioned in disbelief. She pushed past her family and fell at his feet. She was afraid to touch him. His body seemed frail. Searching his eyes, she found a kindle of acquaintance, but she didn't want the pitiful looking man to be her beloved.

"Hello, beautiful," Minton responded, choking up.

His view of her was undisturbed. He suffered from blurred vision and experienced floaters in his line of sight, but Puah was as clear as day. She was older but hadn't aged a bit. She looked healthy and well-manicured. Her hair, still cut short like he liked it, framed her enchanting face. He could tell she drank heavily by the discoloration of her lips, and the fragrant smell of *C. Howard's Purple Violet mints* on her breath. He remembered how they use to suck on three or four at a time to disguise the lingering scent of alcohol. Mags always kept them on her person. The thought of she and Richard's terrible fate stabbed at Minton's heart, and his head fell with sadness.

Overwhelmed, Puah tossed her head into his lap. He smelled of *Old Spice* and an overloading catheter. She wrapped her arms around his feeble legs and wept. She couldn't believe that Minton, the burly lad from Gonzales, was thin enough to carry away. Her entire being cried for him. She felt greater pain than when her parents died.

"I'm sorry, Pu," he apologized, trying to restrain himself from crying which caused him to cough uncontrollably.

Puah stood, acknowledging the stifled cough and wheezing. She was horrified.

What happened?

Lydia offered Minton a napkin from her dinner tray, and he spat blood into it. Noticing one wasn't enough, she offered him another. They all tried not to stare. Against everyone's better judgment, their hearts broke. With every cough Minton sunk deeper into his seat. Slowly, he hunched over himself.

No longer able to withstand the torture, Puah ran off into her bedroom. Other than her whimpering, there was an awkward silence; not from lack of conversation, but heaviness.

"Can I help you?" Lydia finally asked, wondering if Minton passed out.

His head was nearly in his lap. His daughter stood by him, soothing and patting his back. As Lydia approached, she thought she heard Charlotte singing "Leave Me Alone" by *Michael Jackson* under her breath.

"May I have a grocery bag to dispose of this please, sweetheart...and some soapy paper towel for my hands, if possible," Minton answered in a raspy voice.

"I'll take it!" Lydia responded without a second thought, reaching for the napkins.

Rahab and Mr. Jenkins swiftly turned their heads, gawking at her as if to say *are you crazy*. Lydia's servant spirit always looks to accommodate.

"No. I wanna dispose of it myself," Minton insisted. He tightly balled the napkins into his fist, never looking up.

"Okay. I'll bring you a glass of water, too."

Lydia forced herself to push the bad memories aside, and when she reached the kitchen, she beeped Silas using 52*911, which meant hurry up emergency.

Silas had been helping Gomer and Hosea, the newlyweds, move into their Harlem apartment. Somewhere between friendship and the end of high school, something possessed Hosea to ask his longtime friend for her hand in marriage. She'd been rough on herself throughout the years, but Hosea's friendship was constant. Gomer, already angry and resentful from Minton's abandonment, grew jealous of Rahab's success and beauty. She's pretty herself, but self-conscious from past weight issues. Longing for attention, laced with spitefulness toward Rahab and Puah, she became a prostitute.

At first, Gomer begged her sister to give her a chance at dancing in Jeremy's club, but Rahab rejected her wishes. So, Gomer found what she viewed as a success on her own. It turned out she wasn't as great of a dancer as she thought. The streets were more suiting for her.

Hosea thought he put an end to her foolishness. Against the console of his family, church, and friends, the young couple married and quickly became parents to a baby boy they named Jezreel. They lived with Hosea's relatives for a while, but with his smarts and a corporate job, they were able to quickly move out on their own.

"I'm sorry, James. Thank you for everything. Not too many husbands would do this for their wife's ex-man, but I think it's time for us to go," Minton stated, finally lifting his head against his embarrassment. He pulled out a few alcohol wipes from the bag hanging behind his chair and cleaned his hands and around his mouth before facing Mr. Jenkins.

Mr. Jenkins had transferred himself into his favorite reclining chair. Minton couldn't help but feel envious. He was the type of man he wished he'd been. He seemed confident although afflicted, loyal despite their downfalls, kind instead of bitter, and strong in his weakness. Minton found it easy to share his story with him and, without hesitation, Mr. Jenkins invited him home.

Despite the invitation, Minton began to feel he may have been wrong to disrupt their lives again. *It's time to leave. Maybe I'll go see that social worker?* He briefly forgot the power of prayer.

"Daddy, do we have to leave already? What about cake?" the eight-year-old cried. She expected cake from any gathering and Minton usually remembered to bring her *Yodels*. He tugged her gently, directing her on his lap and hugged her tenderly.

"It's alright, Cookie," he said, addressing her by her nickname. "Daddy will get you some cake, I promise."

Charlotte was his sanity, his hope, and his reason for living. Everything he managed to accomplish was for her. Rahab marveled over his sincerity and how tenderly he handled the child. There was a noticeable change in him, beyond physical, which was disturbing. She couldn't begin to figure out how to process the situation, but she knew he had to stay a while longer. Regardless of her feelings, some doors that only he could shut needed closing.

"No, please stay," Rahab interjected, surprising herself. "Besides, Senior..." she managed to push his nickname past her lips. "You haven't seen Si, Go-Go, or your grandkids - Baby Girl and Jez yet."

Minton was dumbfounded. The sound of her voice, now citified, alarmed him. Out of everyone, he knew Rahab would have nothing to do with him. *Wow, she's beautiful. She always has been.* He tried to process her maturity and the information she revealed. *I'm a grandfather?*

Rahab's hair hung loosely down her back in thick black curls. She dressed in early 90's *flyy girl* attire with coordinating platinum and *ice* jewelry adorning her neck, ears, and wrists. A *Movado* watch, long French manicured tips, and *Doc Martens* boots completed her persona. Minton knew exactly the type of guy who claimed her. He used to be that type. He blamed himself for her unfortunate fate and wanted to inform her that hanging from the arm of a drug dealer is beneath her.

"I believe there's still some leftover cake in the fridge. We just celebrated Si and his daughter's birthday a few days ago," Rahab informed, gesturing for Charlotte to follow her into the kitchen.

Minton began to cry openly. He never expected Rahab to treat him with any kindness, furthermore his daughter. *If she spat in my face, I'd feel better.* Her sincerity ushered feelings of unworthiness and shame.

"Thank you," he mouthed, unable to speak.

Rahab's eyes moistened in spite of her attempt to hold back tears. She whispered in Minton's ear. "Let's keep our secret...our secret, for now." She lightly patted his back. She wasn't sure if the statement was for her family's sake or pride's sake. Either way, it was said, and she owned control over the situation. Taking Charlotte by the hand, they started out toward the kitchen.

"What is this, a family reunion?" Jeremy asked, walking into the living room eating peanuts and discarding the shells on the floor. "I hope y'all not trying to move more negroes up in here. You already like roaches."

"Hey, babe," Rahab stated, greeting him warmly. She attempted to hug and kiss him, but he walked past her. Instigating seemed more intriguing.

Jeremy strolled around Minton's wheelchair giving him the once over. "This one's on his way out. What you got homie, AIDS or something?" He laughed at the harsh comments.

The room fell silent. Heads seemed to bow in Jeremy's presence. Minton could feel the tension.

So, this is the jerk.

Jeremy stopped in front of Rahab giving her the death stare. He knew they were up to something. He looked down at Charlotte who was still holding hands with her. All she wanted was cake. She looked up at Jeremy and smiled hard. Her missing teeth and chunky dimpled face ushered a crooked smile from him.

"That's aight, this cutie pie can work the pole for her stay," he cruelly remarked, tousling Charlotte's hair. He was in a particularly evil mood. He grew jealous when family time didn't include him.

"Don't do that," Minton warned. "I may be sick, but I still throw fuh mine." He backed his chair up and sat erect. The bass in his tone resurfaced.

"Jeri, this is Si and Go-Go's dad," Rahab explained, hoping Jeremy would back off. Instead, he laughed. He laughed so vigorously he held his side in pain.

"I know this *Richard Pryor*, *Jo Jo Dancer*, looking mofo didn't just threaten me. Ha! Ya life is sho'nuff calling, homie."

"Babe, don't worry about him. He doesn't matter," Rahab insisted, knowing the language Jeremy liked. "Come on, let's go get you a plate," she added, assuming he was there for dinner.

He shrugged her off and ceased his laughter. Staring Minton down, he closed in on him.

Puah rushed into the living room carrying a warm, covered plate of food in hand. "Look-a-here, Jeri. Lydia made your favorite tonight; rice with stewed oxtails."

She heard Jeremy's voice from her room and remembered Minton's temper was about as fueled as his. She darted into the kitchen and retrieved a plate of food from the oven that Rahab set aside earlier for the men. She hoped he would eat and go or just go.

Jeremy hated to be made a fool of. He knew they were trying to divert his attention, so he slapped the plate out of Puah's hand. The dish shattered into pieces upon hitting the hardwood floor. Charlotte whined.

"No one threatens Jeri Cole." He stands taller, rounding his shoulders.

"Yo, I'm heading out anyway. I have no problem going out fighting," Minton proclaimed, attempting to stand. Puah rested her hand firmly on his shoulder and sat him back down. He was indeed angry, but her warm touch reminded him that he didn't come to make a bad situation worse for his family. He slumped in his seat.

"Ha! Going out fighting," Jeremy repeated. "Old school, I'll bust-a-cap in ya rass. Forget ya whack knuckle game. I'll take you out of your misery," he threatened, slapping him against the head.

Minton grabbed the handrails of his wheelchair and bit down on his lip. *I wish I had my cane. I'd knock the stuffing out of this punk.* He exhaled deeply and recited a prayer within himself. Puah pressed down on his shoulders firmer as Charlotte began to cry.

"Please, Jeri. He's just visiting," Rahab pleads, rubbing his back. "We haven't seen him in years. Please...you're scaring the child," she added, now scratching as he liked.

Jeremy quickly glanced at Charlotte; he could tell she had special needs. There was a secret place in his heart, stemming from childhood, for kids like her.

"I don't wanna see this *dead man* here tomorrow and, for her sake..." he gestured toward Charlotte, "we bet not meet in the streets. I pay for this mofo. Don't any of you moochers forget that! Clean this crap up!" He turned to leave, kicking the shattered china. Rahab followed him to the door promising to come home shortly with his dinner.

BITTERSWEET AFTERTASTE

The slow and drawn out spring day ended in a whirlwind event. Minton's abandonment was hard enough to deal with on its own; his resurrection left a bittersweet taste in their mouths.

Silas rushed into the apartment nearly thirty minutes after he received the beep from Lydia. Everyone was still gathered in the living room talking. No one noticed when he arrived. He stood at the entry of the living room with his hands tossed in the air staring at Lydia as if to say *what's the deal?* He advised them to only use the 52*911 beep for extreme emergencies at home.

"Ay, hola, Papi," Lydia expressed in an uneasy tone. She noticed the aggravation in Silas' eyes, so she carefully turned Minton's wheelchair around to face him. "Look. It's your dad," she revealed, not sure of how to break the mind-boggling news.

Silas' knees buckled. He braced himself against the arched entryway and held his chest as he turned three shades lighter.

Minton stared at his son, full of pride. *Ain't he a sight for sore eyes.*

Silas was tall and handsome, caught somewhere between Puah's unblemished charm and his rugged good looks. His hair, still firmly packed and full of thick, lustrous, black curls was cut lower than his childhood high-top fade. He wasn't the lanky boy Minton remembered. He had facial hair, and his shoulders were broad and muscular. His body was long and firm.

"Junior!" Minton shouted, cheerfully. He wanted to stand and embrace his namesake, but he could only manage to stand in spirit. "Silas. My boy." He extended his arms.

Silas was in disbelief. His heart leaped from his chest like during the initial drop of a thrill ride. He felt both excited and betrayed. Minton looked like an actual corpse and he already mentally grieved his passing. *There's no way Senior's alive.*

"No." Silas wanted to crawl within himself like a snail. "My father is dead."

"I'm sorry, son," Minton responded, feeling defeated. He allowed his hands to fall back into his lap. He knew his return was no happy reunion, but he kept setting himself up for a celebration. *They have the right to hate me.*

"Sorry for what?" Silas queried, sucking up his tears. His complexion changed from pale to red. He paced the hall arguing with himself. "Sorry, pfft! That's it. I hate sorries. Sorry is a sad excuse. That's what it is! Sorry for what...returning after almost nine years. For what? To die on us."

Minton bowed his head. There were no words of comfort, means of peace, nor reason for forgiveness. He was dying, and no one had the guts to ask. Silas knew instantly. He lived and breathed in the city streets during the epidemic. He knew the AIDS virus when he saw it.

"Yes, son. It's true. I am dying," Minton confirmed to sniffling, wailing, and moaning coming from his family.

Silas gaped at his estranged father for a moment before turning to leave. He intended upon remaining indignant, but Minton's affirmation of his illness aroused various emotions. Silas' feet headed for the door, but his heart turned him around. He swiftly entered the living room and impulsively scooped Minton up into a bear hug. Then allowed himself to fall apart completely. He cried, maybe harder than a man should, but enough for the boy left without a father. Constrained, Minton rested his head against his son's stiff shoulder and thanked the Lord. *There's no place better than the warmth of a genuine hug.* They consumed the moment.

"I love you, Senior, but I...I just don't know. Why would you come back like this?" Silas cried, attempting to express his feelings while Puah, Lydia, and Rahab worked on loosening his grip from around Minton's frail body.

"Sit him down, beb," Puah asked, but Silas' mind was elsewhere.

"Put him down, son!" Mr. Jenkins demanded.

Silas slowly released his father.

Their glistening eyes locked. Minton was more than a corpse. Silas saw repentance, shame, significant pain, and loneliness. He instinctively knew what he'd been through and the past didn't matter anymore. His father needed him.

"It's okay, Dad. It's okay." Silas firmly gripped Minton's shoulders and hunched over him. "I'm going to take care of you now," he assured his father, feeling the need to liberate him of worry. Minton covered his face and released his tears. Finally feeling free.

JC MILLER

WHEN THE STREETS CALL

There was a period of time when Silas answered the call of the streets. Yes, you can say he knew the demons his father fought. They launched a personalized battle against him which ultimately humbled him into understanding. After years of looking down on the addicts he questioned while searching for Minton, he became that which he hunted. Betrayed by integrity. Stripped of willpower. Silas fell captive to the lure of comforters and lust. The underworld surfaced quickly. He rationalized it as the bounty of success and wallowed in its corruption.

With Jeremy came women, money, and drugs. He ordered Silas around like one of his stooges and quickly took over managing Rahab's career, eliminating Silas' protection.

"I don't need any leeches sucking money from me! My name is her bodyguard, and my squad is tight," Jeremy declared condescendingly. He didn't want influences hanging around his investment. "Either you work for me in Brooklyn, wholeheartedly, or step off."

Jeremy knew Rahab esteemed her brother and disliked the idea of a dominating male figure hanging around. He was the alpha male. So, he plotted Silas' move. Once relocated, Jeremy's partners under no affiliation would bribe Silas with money and free drug samples. Then offer him opportunities to make *fast cash*. Jeremy, a cold-blooded pro, knew Silas' track record. He perceived him as a sloppy runner, driven by emotions and weak in spirit. Ultimately, he'd end up arrested, addicted, or dead. He set Silas up for failure expecting the latter.

I AM RAHAB

    Silas promised himself that he would never sell drugs again, but he unexpectedly found himself craving the material possessions flaunted around him. He accepted Jeremy's offer and, along with Lydia and their daughter, Krystal, they moved from under his family's guidance.

    He rented a studio apartment from Jeremy and paid the landlord, who was also the boss, the salary he earned. Silas enjoyed the respect his appearance demanded as a bouncer, but he wasn't in love with Jeremy's financial hold over his pockets. His situation made it hard to turn down the offer his new friends propositioned. They cut him in on small deals and threw him a few dollars, *dime bags,* and loose women. Like good friends, they helped him and Lydia move into a larger apartment. They celebrated with bottles of *Cristal* and lines of coke until finally hooking him on the lifestyle. Lydia, caught up in the whirlwind and accustomed to mirroring Silas, enjoyed the ride. She ate in fancy restaurants, attended lavish parties, wore the latest apparel, and *blew* a few lines herself. It was easy transitioning Silas over to freebase crack cocaine. Soon, the dealer became his own customer. He stopped showing up for work, owed money and was behind in rent. A familiar Williams tale. If it wasn't for Lydia's love and resilience, Silas' story might have taken a deadly turn.

    Lydia reluctantly confided in Rahab with the details of their existence. The young women briefly lost the endearment of their relationship in the shuffle of that year's events. They acquainted, from time to time, attending industry parties, doing work for Jeremy, and family functions. During the last party they attended, Rahab questioned Lydia about Silas' well-being, noticing the obvious difference in his behavior and appearance.

Lydia was ashamed and hid their conduct. Their actions weren't any worse than the family's sordid affairs, but she expected more from herself. Under Silas' addiction, they'd lost everything. Lydia and Krystal were secretly sleeping in shelters. When Lydia hadn't heard from Silas for over a week, she broke down and called Rahab to meet her.

No love was lost between the blood sisters as they embraced and cried in each other's arms. Rahab paid off her brother's street debt, questioning pushers while in search of him. No one let on of his whereabouts, they just implied that he was around. Reassured that Silas was still living, Lydia requested that Rahab take Krystal home to the Bronx and allow her and Silas to correct the situation alone. They'd gotten themselves into it; they just needed a little time to recover. If she needed the family, she'd call.

During Lydia's stay in the shelter, she befriended a den mother who was also a local pastor's daughter. Den Mother Paula noticed Lydia's distant and anxious behavior. She sat alone biting her nails and, aside from proper salutations, didn't converse with the other women. One day, during a brief encounter that kindled a lasting friendship, Paula suggested that Lydia start to pray.

"Speak to the Lord of all creation," she boldly advised in a plainspoken kind of way as if Lydia should have known. "There's no reason you should ever be anxious about anything. *For every animal of the forest is His, and the livestock on a thousand hills,*" she delightfully proclaimed to Lydia's confusion.

"Whaa?" Lydia asked perplexed.

Paula sweetly smiled and began explaining how everything belonged to God. She insisted that Lydia communicate with this father who loved her unconditionally through prayer and supplication.

"Let your requests be made known unto God," Paula advised. "Then you will experience His peace, which exceeds anything we can understand. His peace will guard your heart and your thoughts in Christ Jesus."

Although she didn't understand, Lydia decided to put *this faith* into practice. Her trips to the Botánica with Puah were useless. Den Mother Paula seemed at peace while Puah fought against the world. It seemed Señora Martha only foresaw trouble and suggested costly antidotes. Paula's peace was free. Lydia began regularly attending Sunday and mid-week services. She learned of God's burning love for her.

At first, it was hard to accept that the creator of the universe would care for a short Puerto Rican reject from the South Bronx. Choosing to continue worrying and picking up pieces seemed rational. Lydia acquired employment at a local fast food restaurant and attended the *Fashion Institute of Technology* on tuition assistance and grants. The more she relied on herself, the more she worried. The more she believed and prayed on her and Silas' behalf, the more she experienced random and unexpected blessings. She was blessed with an apartment in Canarsie along with a roommate to keep her company. A professor gave her a used sewing machine that she quickly put to use branding *Lydia's Purple Palace*. Then, multiple offers to help with fashion shows affiliated with the school emerged out of nowhere. Lydia started to design costumes for the strippers at Jeremy's clubs, making sure to always add her signature color of purple in some intricate manner. She also haphazardly began evangelizing to them. In the short time spent in Brooklyn, she paved the beginnings of a lucrative career.

Between trials and triumphs, Lydia noticed the hand of the Lord. Her mental outlook changed as well as her heart for Christ. As evidence of her surrender, she was baptized.

One evening while she sat alone working on some outfits in a shop class, she broke down crying. Because of her faithfulness, the Lord was blessing her in every way but one. He hadn't brought Silas back, but Lydia knew he was okay. He called home whenever he was in a bind, and Puah and Rahab immediately wired money.

"Lydia's looking for you," they would relay to his grunts of disapproval. Each time they offered her number, and each time Silas suggested she forget about him, which was impossible. You can't forget the air you breathe.

Feeling distressed, Lydia humbly cried out to the Lord. She was grateful for everything, but *everything* meant nothing if Silas' soul was lost. Silas saved *her life* when her life's outlook was grim. Even if he didn't return to her, she prayed for his salvation.

In the midst of prayer, Lydia heard an inner voice say, **"He's in a crack house in Bedford Stuyvesant."**

Lydia beat the pavement in *Do or Die Bed Stuy* until she found her beloved. Declaring and decreeing God's perfect will over his life, she literally willed Silas' body and mind out of captivity. In the middle of a crack house with his back leaned against a dirty tagged up wall she professed that his life was foreordained for God's eternal purpose and glory. She sealed the statement, "In Jesus' name."

Silas, still high, gawked at his Bucky Le-Le and laughed inwardly. The more he considered an invisible god loving and creating him, the more he laughed. An intense burst of laughter spilled over the perceived useless notion.

He didn't feel the subtle yet powerful jolt of the covering proclaimed over him. He didn't acknowledge the events and people placed strategically on his path maneuvering and aligning him with God's will.

Lydia grabbed Silas by the ear and pulled him out of the gutter. She dragged him to *Kings County Hospital Center's Detoxification drug rehab* and threatened his life if he didn't stay put. He completed the program only to fall victim to the streets again. Every time he fell, Lydia prayed and found him. She did the same thing each time, never wavering from her quest for God's perfect will over his life. Each time, Silas released the same hearty laughter.

Early one cold morning between crack houses and detox, Silas was called upon by a building contractor soliciting day laborers on the same corner he was loitering in East New York.

"Hey, you, buddy!" the man shouted, startling Silas from sleep. "You wanna make some hard-earned cash today?" He lightly kicked Silas against his foot to wake him up.

The man noticed him nodding off against a bodega wall surrounded by the usual Mexicans that were there ready to work. He could tell Silas was a user, but he couldn't take his eyes off him. He was a baby in the streets. The man felt a nudge in his spirit to pick him up.

"...and then what, Lord?" the man quietly asked.

"...*and then my will*," the Lord proclaimed.

"Do you wanna make some hard-earned cash today?" the man repeated as Silas fully awakened.

Confused and in pain he answered, "Yeah, why not."

Silas joined the others in a white van. The workers spoke amongst themselves in Spanish, wondering about him. They had come prepared with carpenter bags full of tools of the trade. Silas sat bewildered, tucked in a corner for the first twenty minutes of the ride. For the next fifteen minutes, he wondered which tools would bring him the most profit on the streets. He'd set his eyes on a woodworker's toolbox by the time the van arrived at a *Long Island* property.

"What's your name, buddy?" the man asked, handing Silas a brown bag containing two buttered bagels and black coffee.

"Minton Williams," Silas answered, providing his *government name*.

"Okay, well eat up, Minton. You got a long day ahead of you. I'm Paul," he stated in a thick Brooklyn accent, extending his hand. "I build houses."

Neither man anticipated the friendship. They worked closely that day. Paul, mostly observing, wanted to see where he could place Silas. Silas was no handyman, but he was still strong and good with numbers. Amid their summing up of one another, they engaged in conversation. As the day progressed, Paul could tell that Silas was getting antsy.

His last fix was four days ago. On that particular day, a robbery went astray. Silas attempted to rob a man but instead of getting any money, he got a *beat down* by his victim and his victim's crew. They left him for dead in a back alley. For two days he laid there in and out of consciousness. No one came to his rescue; no one cared. Against the pain of his bruised ribs, he finally found the strength to sit up adjacent to the building behind him. He noticed a brown paper bag marked *"for you."* It contained a hero, *quarter water*, and a warm cup of black coffee. Silas surveyed the area back and forth before gobbling down the food and drinks. By the evening of the third day, he managed to walk to the corner. He badly wanted a fix, but he couldn't muster the energy to walk let alone rob someone, and the payphone to call home was two blocks away. Silas sat on the corner near a bodega begging passersby for money. Around eight o'clock that night, a woman threw him a bag of chips as she exited the store and ran to her car. Insulted, he painfully threw them back. When the store's owner tried to sweep him away, he explained he'd hit his head and needed a little time. He gave Silas water and told him to leave by morning. Around midnight, some young folks around his age walked by laughing at him. One even spat in his face. Silas was feeling better and clear-minded enough to know he had had enough of this living. Around three in the morning, hungry, craving drugs, and missing his family, he looked up beyond the street light and prayed, "God, if you're real…get me home. Then, I'll believe in you." He then fell asleep.

    Silas ended up staying in Paul's garage for a few days, against his daughter's nagging. Appreciative of the day's work and conversation, Silas asked that he not be paid. Instead, he asked for food and shelter; Paul agreed. Silas knew if he were paid he would only buy drugs. Since he managed not to rob any of his co-workers, he convinced himself he could stay clean as long as he remained out of the hood.

    Paul asked his daughter for assistance regarding privately owned detoxification programs. He felt with the proper guidance Silas had a chance at recovery. Against her better judgment, she gave him a list of organizations he could afford. She loved her father and was concerned that he was in over his head. He'd lost his wife, her mother, a little over a year ago and was still very vulnerable. Nevertheless, Silas entered a recovery program and six months later emerged a new man.

Proud of Silas' achievement, Paul invited him, along with his daughter, to a celebratory steak dinner. His daughter was instantly impressed with the handsome young man her father brought home. They sat for a long while engaged in small talk. After dinner and before dessert, they discovered Minton, as they called him, preferred to be called Si, short for Silas, and he belonged to their Lydia.

Lydia had been attending Pastor Paul's East New York church for a year and her friend, Den Mother Paula, was his daughter. She'd spoken of Silas numerous times, but Paula never linked them. They all wrote it off as God's will and the young couple reunited.

They finally married and brought Krystal back to Brooklyn to live with them. Silas was baptized under Pastor Paul's church and continued building houses with him. Lydia finished school, earning her associate degree in fashion design and continued gaining success creating purple inspired designs. They eventually moved back to the Bronx with their family in Jeremy's building because Silas caught wind that Jeremy may have been abusing Rahab.

INVITED TO STAY

Silas can say he understands his father's struggles and the sweat, blood, and tears it takes to resurface after dwelling in the depths of addiction. He knows all too well the downward spiral of a misplaced existence, and he thanks God daily for his second chance.

"Bugs! Pull out the sofa bed, Senior's back," Silas ordered happily, glad for the opportunity to see Minton again no matter the situation. "That's if it's alright by Pops," he added, remembering Mr. Jenkins outranked him. He filled Minton's shoes long ago, and they respected and loved him.

"I already invited him to stay," Mr. Jenkins answered, saluting Minton with a power fist as he smiled and wheeled his chair out of the living room. His job was complete, and all he desired was a hot shower and dessert in bed while watching *The Tonight Show with Jay Leno*. Then later, if his wife ever came to bed, a hot date to fall asleep near while listening to her watch *David Letterman* and local programming, as usual. However, he sensed, tonight would be different.

"Night all!" he yelled back to his dysfunctional family.

JC MILLER

CLOSURE

"I'm a disappointment, aren't I?" Minton declares of himself, struggling from his wheelchair so he can lie in the comfortable looking bed Lydia prepared for him. He wouldn't care if it were a pallet on the floor. It feels good to be amongst family, but he can sense Puah's distance.

"I can't say you're a grand prize," she truthfully responds, snapping from a trance. She quickly assists Minton with getting into bed. Her touch sends shivers up his spine.

"Would it be out of line to ask for your company for a while?" he questions, wanting to feel her presence a little longer.

"No, of course," Puah answers, helping him to bed and tucking him in. She lies on top of the comforter near him and rests her head on his chest. It's more than Minton expected. He instinctively plays with her damp hair. It still smells of coconut.

"So, what's the verdict? What is it that you have?" Puah queries, not feeling like beating around the bush any longer. The initial shock is over, and she's ready to speak candidly.

They all assume he has *acquired immunodeficiency syndrome,* but she wants clarification. Her time spent with Minton was high-risk, but she knows she's negative. She and Mr. Jenkins tested for *STDs* before marriage and again when he needed a transfusion after the shooting. Her questioning is simply out of curiosity.

"I have KS...*Epidemic Kaposi Sarcoma.* It's *AIDS*-related cancer," Minton reveals, feeling a sharp pain in his chest like multiple stab wounds directed toward his heart.

He closes his eyes and exhales through his mouth, pushing past the pain. He's on a mission, and he's come too far to die before it's complete.

"So how long do you have?" Puah asks, cutting to the chase.

"I don't know…a month…a week, maybe any day," Minton answers, not intending to scare her or commence her to crying again but wishing to be as honest as possible.

The truth is, a week ago his doctors were counseling him on discontinuing chemotherapy and entering hospice.

He developed full-blown *AIDS* a year or so after Charlotte's mother passed from the same diagnosis. When she died, he began making plans for Charlotte's future. He spoke to a few professionals about placement programs for children with special needs, and a working proposal was in motion, but nothing felt right. He kept putting off finalizing the paperwork. When his doctor suggested entering hospice and gave him a definite timeline of demise, he decided to get in touch with his family. He promised himself not to interfere with their lives but hearing the totality of his life was at its end twisted his arm toward reuniting. He went home and packed a backpack with essential documents, a few items of clothing, Charlotte's toothbrush, a few pictures, an envelope full of money, and his Bible. Everything else in the small apartment was, in the end, just things. Minton headed for *Harlem* and didn't turn back.

Puah sighs profoundly and rises from the bed. She heads for a fully loaded black lacquered bar, catty-cornered against the wall. With her back turned, she asks if he wants a drink.

"No, thank you." Minton is aware of her frustration.

"Why not? You're dying anyway. One drink won't hurt." She felt spiteful and grieved at the same time. *Why did he have to resurface? My Casanova and prince.* She chokes up and covers her mouth as tears the size of raindrops roll from her eyes.

"I'm sorry, Pu," Minton apologizes, hearing her sniveling. "I know this isn't fair to you and the kids. Please come back and lay next to me. Leave the drink, let's talk soberly," he appeals, feeling the sharp pain again.

His spirit reminds him to be encouraged in spite of his breaking heart. **Healing is in the process.**

Puah leaves the crystal snifter glass of peach brandy and sits on the edge of the sofa bed. Her blurry gaze fixates on the abandoned drink. She wants to guzzle away any memories of the past four hours.

"Pu," Minton speaks, freeing her from her daze. She turns her head slightly, granting him her attention. "You know, I've been praying to God for an opportunity for closure with you and the kids."

Puah sucks her teeth and rolls her eyes, turning back toward the drink. She doesn't want to hear anything about God. The God of promises, the God of hope. Lydia and Silas preach of Him enough. There is no God as far as she's concerned. She's done with false hope and higher beings.

"I know you don't want to hear it, but God has answered my prayers. He—"

"What happened, Senior? Why did you leave us like that?" Puah doesn't want answers from God. She needs answers from Minton. She lies across his legs facing him and props her hand under her chin giving him complete attention. "Tell me what happened. I need to know."

"I just figured everyone would be better off without me," Minton answers, staring her in the eyes. It's a simple truth.

"Oh, is that what you thought?" Puah says, patronizing him.

Minton pauses for a moment trying to gather his thoughts. Although it feels like yesterday, years have passed, and he's lost his reasoning.

"When I left you guys, I was in the worst place I've ever been mentally." He wants to cry, but he's taught himself to hold back. Puah can tell he's broken. "I'm dying of AIDS, and this pain isn't greater than what I felt the night I left. I had intentions of committing suicide. I didn't want to live without you, but I was no good for you."

"So, you decided to start another family instead?" she presumes, judging despite his pain. "For Pete's sake, Cookie and Krystal are the same age. You didn't waste any time forgetting us."

"That's not true," Minton assures her, shaking his head no. "I've never forgotten my family. I've lived in torture for over eight years, not forgetting."

"Well, that's something we both can relate to."

"Not that it makes any difference, but I don't know if Cookie is even mine," he whispers, so as not to allow anyone else to hear his *man-card rejecting* statement. Minton sips a drink of water. This is the first time in a long time he's had this much energy. "The night I left Rah's party, my intentions were to get one last high then kill myself, but when I got to *The Palace*, I noticed my friend...this prostitute that I was helping out...well, we were helping each other out..." He attempts to clarify but stumbles for words trying to explain Samantha to Puah.

Their relationship was complicated. Minton loved Samantha as best he could and made life comfortable for her and Charlotte. She never felt like a replacement even though she was. The problem was, she loved the streets. She was the reason he was in the predicament he's in, although it's surprising that he didn't contract the virus first.

Minton notices Puah twisting her lips in suspicion, so he tries again to clarify his relationship with Samantha during the time he and Puah were together. "I used to provide a place for her to stay, my work van, and she in return used to bring me *fixes*."

"Umhmm, what else did she fix?"

"Of course, there was sex involved," he adds, remembering he and Puah have both moved on. "Anyway she, Sam, had overdosed. She was slumped over in a corner and I couldn't wake her up. I asked for help, but no one moved. So, I pulled her out by the arms and flagged the first police car I saw. To make a long story short, spending time with her on the brink of death brought me life. I decided that if she lived, I would live and maybe we could help each other clean up. When she pulled through, we sort of became each other's support. Listen, Pu, you're a beautiful woman. I felt like with me out of your way, you all would have a better chance at life," Minton declares sincerely. Knowing now that may not have been the best decision. "Sam found out she was pregnant while in the hospital…and to be honest, we were happy. It gave us both an incentive to detox. HIV came later when she couldn't stay out of the streets. Cookie was born with Down syndrome, and Sam blamed herself. She wanted to hand her over to the state, but I convinced her that I would take on the responsibility of being Cookie's father," he adds, hunching his shoulders gesturing that he's not sure if he is the child's father or not. "We moved to *Red Hook*. I worked at a car wash and when Sam finally got off the streets she cleaned office buildings. We did what we had to do...you know?"

Puah is quiet, and Minton isn't sure how to read that. He continues his story in spite of her silence knowing he needs to drive home *the big request*. "But, my Cookie is a good kid, Pu." He smiles, thinking of Charlotte. "All she does is watch videos, sing, and dance all day. There is one thing though...I call it M-J-itis."

"What's that?" Puah asks with concern. Charlotte reminds her of Gomer as a child. How Minton can have any reservations about DNA is beyond her. *It's obvious.*

"She's liable to sudden outbursts of *Michael Jacksonisms*," Minton continues, laughing. "She sings and reenacts his videos throughout the day. She even speaks *Michael* at times."

Puah begins to laugh too. That explains the movements she was making while gulping down her cake earlier.

"Sha'mone! That means come on," Minton explains.

"Stop lying on that child, Senior," Puah laughs, tickled.

"I kid you not." He crosses his heart. "Hee-hee! That means yes. *Mama-say mama-sa mama-coo-sa;* I haven't figured that one out yet. It's multifaceted," he laughs, filling Puah in on his daughter's silly habits. "She's brought me so much joy! I'm sure you can relate with our grandkids being born and all," he adds, a little more serious. Thinking of leaving Charlotte is harder than he imagined.

"You don't have to sell her to me; she's a sweet kid," Puah responds, making up in her mind that whatever happened, happened. They all moved on. "She must have been a lot of work with the both of you being sick. Did you have help? Does she have family?" Puah inquisitively asks.

"Sadly, no. Sam never spoke much about her family besides her being from Cleveland and the fact that she used to be a student at *NYU* that's all I know of her past. They disowned her is all she shared."

"What's going to happen to Cookie when you're gone?" Puah questions, now concerned.

"Well, I was kinda hoping that's where you come in," he admits, glad to finally have the request off of his chest.

"Wait, hold up!" Puah shouts, sitting up. "You mean to tell me the only reason you came back was to make me a babysitter?"

"No, Pu," Minton interjects, realizing how shady it sounded.

"You know, Minton; you still ain't sh—"

"Pu! Hear me out. Come on, babe." He lowers her pointed finger. She crosses her arms and legs Indian style and pouts.

"Come on, Pu. Lay back down, please. Let's talk this over. That came out wrong."

Minton rubs Puah's shoulder trying to calm her down. Angry, she falls backward with her legs and arms still crossed. Minton snickers, remembering her hot temper. *She's even more beautiful angry.* He wishes he can feel her lips against his again.

"Go ahead, clean it up," she insists.

"I love you guys; there's no doubt about that. You *are* my family and you don't know how many times I've wanted to check in on you all, but I promised myself that I wouldn't ruin your lives again. I have AIDS; what do I have to offer?" He uncrosses her arms and takes her hand. "I was wrong for how I handled everything...I'm sorry." Puah's eyes start to fill again as he continues.

Why is he so darn sincere all of a sudden? She is irritated by her inability to stay mad at him.

"When Sam died, I was left alone with Cookie and didn't know what to do. Because I was older, I always assumed I would go first. I felt maybe she would connect with her family again and that would be that. I didn't plan it this way, Pu, but yes, I do want my daughter to be with my family," he declares as tears roll down Puah's cheeks. She can't believe this is happening. "I NEVER stopped loving you," Minton reveals. "You will always be my *Saturday Love*." He smiles down at her, referring to an *Alexander O'Neal* and *Cherrelle* song. Puah snivels and grins, remembering the older song as their anthem. "I never stopped wanting to see you, wanting to dance with you, wanting to hear your laughter, hold you at night...wanting to..." Minton stops himself. Those thoughts are useless; *there's no point in stirring them up.*

Puah begins to bawl. "I never stopped loving you either, Senior," she reveals, whimpering. "I physically moved on, but mentally I never left you." She crawls back into his arms. "You're my *only* love."

They shed tears in silence, revisiting abandoned possibilities and replaying their anthem from the back of their minds.

Puah abruptly rises to her knees, clearing her face of tears. She's hastily decided that if Minton dies, she's going with him into the afterworld. She pulls her nightgown over her head revealing her new curvaceous body. Partially naked, she lies across his chest.

"What! What are you doing, woman?" Minton stutters completely caught off guard. A warm and fuzzy feeling awakens inside of him.

"I don't want to live without you; I can't. Look at me!" Puah yells, holding his face steadily toward hers.

"Shhh," Minton hushes her, afraid that her nonsense will awaken the sleeping family. She lowers her voice.

"Listen, I drink and smoke way too much. I'm angry and bitter most days and crazy the others, and it's all because I don't belong here." Puah is now straddled on top of the comforters that cover him. "A part of me is missing, and it's you. I may as well die with you because I can't *do this* again," she cries, no longer viewing Minton as a walking corpse but the love of her life. She lowers to kiss him.

Once upon a time, when passion trumped morals, and common sense was an afterthought, all caution would have been tossed to the wind. Minton purses his lips together and attempts to push her aside.

Frustrated and disappointed, Puah releases her tight grip on his face. He turns his head, aiming not to look at her. All he can think about is Mr. Jenkins and how kind he's been toward him. *This is my day of reckoning.* Minton gathers himself as he closes his eyes and pushes the feelings he still has for her deeper within himself. His hands itch to touch her.

Puah stares at the side of his face a moment longer before unmounting. She knows it's crazy, but she longs to feel his body no matter his afflictions. *I'll kill myself afterward and spare the pain of losing him.*

"Puah Marie Auguste, you are beautiful," Minton emphasizes, facing her. Tears roll from his eyes as he ponders the kind of love she must have for him to consider giving her life away. *The life I desire to keep.* He sums it up as God-love. *For God so loved the world that He gave. What a selfish coward I've been.*

"Pu, you saved our family." She turns her back to him. "Listen to me; you're a she-ro. Your love is…it's more than words, it's sacrificial."

"Then why won't you sacrifice and kiss me, touch me, something, anything!" she sobs loudly, needing comfort.

Minton looks at her smooth, caramel-colored back and runs his cold hand down her warm arm. His lustful feelings have languished and his heart breaks for her. His life is hanging in the balance of another realm, but Puah's soul needs saving.

"I learned a long time ago that you can't live on impulse alone. Feelings are temporary and cause a lot of trouble. They rob life from underneath you. You have a good husband that loves you; he can give you far more than I ever did."

"That's not true; you gave me far more," Puah sobs. "Yes, James is a wonderful man and a steady provider, but I don't love him like this. I never did. He knows that. This is crazy love; I'd die for you," she insists, looking back at Minton.

"My heart…is so full listening to you say these things and I wish that I'd heard you before, now I'm dead and no good to anyone," he answers, still talking to her back. "If you don't hear another word that I say, hear this. Please LIVE. Live for the kids. Live for Rah; she needs you more than you know. This world that she's living in, it isn't real. Get out of this apartment and away from that hustler."

Puah sucks her teeth and turns facing him. Her eyes are red from crying. "You don't know what you're talking about; it's complicated."

Minton tries to focus on her face and not her perfectly beautiful body.

"It doesn't matter how hard life gets, you have each other and in the end, trust me, that's all that matters." His eyes drift. "Being amongst my family is all...I...want. Pu, please put some clothes on, you killin' me, ma!"

"Can I dance for you like I used to?" she teases, standing up on the mattress.

"No!" Respect and honor, he owes that to Mr. Jenkins.

Puah slips back into her gown and hops off the bed. She heads for her drink.

"You don't need that."

"Ha! You wrong about that, jack."

Puah gulps down the brandy with her back turned, not wanting Minton to see her gluttony.

"That numbness leads to death. It's the kiss of the enemy, can't you see? Look at me, Pu!"

She turns around annoyed and sees that Minton has removed his shirts. Open lesions cover his chest. Puah can't help but drop her glass.

"LIVE, PU! You're more than this."

Minton lived for another month after his return and gave each day one-hundred percent of himself. Every morning that he was granted breath, he thanked God and humbly asked for the opportunity to enjoy his *time* with his family. Each day, his family found the strength they needed to deal with his illness through his hearty laughter and determination to live. Puah and Silas insisted that Minton stay with them as opposed to a hospice facility.

She sobered up and took charge, lovingly taking on the task of caring for her diminishing ex as he affectionately received the chance to watch her and Charlotte cling to one another. Minton met his grandchildren and reconciled with Gomer, who, unlike the others, instantly forgave her father. She reclaimed her title as Princess Go-Go and fought Puah and Charlotte at every corner for his attention. She wasn't fond of the idea of having a younger sister, but regardless of Gomer's feelings for Charlotte, Minton, Puah, and Mr. Jenkins started custody paperwork. Mr. Jenkins assured Minton that it would be his pleasure to adopt Charlotte.

"This family of misfits belongs together. You family, too, bro. No kin left behind," Mr. Jenkins declared.

On the day that Minton passed, the women decided to prepare him the good old-fashioned meal he'd been reminiscing about. They propped him up in his wheelchair with his legs elevated at the table and bundled him in blankets. He laughed and dozed as the women cooked, joked, danced, and joyfully prepared him a meal he wasn't able to enjoy. Shrimp and sausage jambalaya, barbecued baby back ribs, mixed greens with ham hocks, baked macaroni and cheese, potato salad, New Orleans style bread pudding with rum butter sauce, and Lydia's famous pernil he'd heard so much about were on the menu. He reflectively smiled watching Puah teach the girls how to hustle while listening to *Kiss FM's DJ Tony Humphries Mastermix Dance Party*. Growing tired of Puah and Minton's beloved house music, Rahab switched stations and taught them to do the *Rump Shaker* to *Wreckx-N-Effect* while listening to no other than DJ Jay-Skii Money's Midday Mix. Minton laughed and nearly coughed up a lung at Lydia trying to keep up. They all agreed that she should sit down before she killed him.

"It's not my fault, the music is all wrong," Lydia insisted, switching to *La Mega 97.9,* a Spanish language radio station. She called for Silas, and the two showed off their *Salsa* to *Celia Cruz's* "Azúcar Negra." Silas shocked everyone with his well-maneuvered techniques and Lydia smiled wide, gracefully dancing in sync with him. Puah yelled for Mr. Jenkins and the kids. They all crowded the kitchen dancing and eating.

The smile on Minton's face will forever be etched in their memories as he closed his eyes to doze eternally. He felt no contempt in his heart nor doubt in his mind when his spirit passed on quietly. He knew that whatever they lacked, God would provide and, by and by, they all would unite in glory.

THE LAND OF MILK AND HONEY

JC MILLER

BONNIE AND CLYDE

If you're not careful, time has a way of vanishing your existence. Who you were becomes a vague memory. Rahab wasn't a victim of circumstance. Wanting a taste of the *Land of Milk and Honey*, she naively allowed Jeremy to mold her, to steal her identity and contaminate her dreams with his own.

Once upon a time, she thought dancing was all she wanted. It wasn't. It's the freedom that dance allows that she craves. Hungry for security and fame, she foolishly worked for Jeremy for six years believing that he held her dreams in his hand, but she was the answer to his triumph. His clubs, Vixen and Vixen 2.0, are more prosperous now than they've ever been, and their success stems from Rahab's hard work under Jeremy's venomous management firm, Island Boy Promotions. She was the first client and star. Her attractiveness and talent allotted her the fame she sought but, like a puppeteer, Jeremy's hand was up her back.

Jeremy managed Rahab's career as promised, taking her from mediocre *pole success* to budding fame. She featured in, as well as choreographed, popular music videos, stage performances, and off-Broadway productions. She was *that girl* that young women dream of being. The temptress *dressed to the nines* and draped on the arm of a favorite celebrity. It was part of her job description. She did the videos then allowed the paparazzi to do the rest. Voodoo Doll was a hot commodity in the late 80's and early 90's hip-hop and rap community. Rumors linking her with *this* artist or *that* rapper kept her valid. Her appearances and affiliation with the culture lured both men and women to Jeremy's clubs. He used her like *Kleenex*. She became the brand he marketed; sex. Voodoo Doll was the face of a new era, and Island Boy Promotions managed her deals and collected her checks.

"Wah yuh need funds fa? I'm your debit card," Jeremy insists whenever she asks about her money, reckoning he keeps her *up to par*.

Rahab's always lavishly dressed. Jeremy's cars are her cars. His *cribs* are her *cribs*. She wants for nothing. The only money she touches is what she makes behind the scenes selling Big Mama's beauty products. Jeremy's dominating behavior frustrates her, but she never questions him. She believes that he has their best interests at heart. Not only does he take care of her, but against Mr. Jenkins' liking, he makes sure that Puah and Charlotte are well kept in their lavishly decorated basement apartment.

Three years into Rahab's popularity, Jeremy somewhat randomly, but not entirely surprising, severed all of her external affairs and ended her career. In spite of the money, he grew jealous and feared she'd rise and rebel against him. So, he banished her from the public eye.

"You're becoming too accessible, mon," he claimed, sucking his tongue through his teeth. "You're the main course, like oxtails o'va rice-n-peas and a likkle salad inna di side. You ain't no appetizer," he stated, justifying her early retirement. He insisted that she solely focus on duplicating herself. "Become a *boss* and less a slave."

So instead of being the star, Voodoo Doll began grooming young women into lucrative mini-clones of herself. Jeremy's plan was strategic. He did what Rahab does on stage. He gave the city a taste and then drew her back, promising more. It's no surprise his scheme worked; the shock was how quickly it took off.

In spite of Jeremy's controlling ways, he and Rahab work well together. They stake-out clubs, sipping on *Dom Perignon* in VIP and pointing out prominent females. The pretty girls, only there to score men with deep pockets don't dance much but they've mastered the game of allurement. Those women, along with girls from modeling agencies, casting couches, other strip clubs, struggling college students, and a few *hood starz* are the ones they bring in for auditions. A chosen few become *Jeri's Video Vixens*. He subtly transitions them into working as escorts, prostitutes, boom-boom room girls, porn stars, and pin-ups. There are no warning signs or reasons to feel suspicious. He promises fame, and he delivers. But fame costs. His tactics are aggressive and usually involve bad contracts, drugs, blackmail, and manipulation. Some girls only make it as far as stripping; others showcase in popular music videos and rub elbows with the stars. Jeremy's personal favorites are the pin-up girls and porn stars. They're golden. Without hesitating, they do anything and everything he asks. Ultimately, all the girls work for him, and the magic behind all of it is their accessibility to the public. Seeing your *dream girl* perform live is only a token and a short train ride away. Better yet, for the right price, you can buy the night of your dreams.

Jeri's Video Vixens work the poles along with the usual strippers, but twice a week they perform video showcases featuring Rahab's choreography that lures large audiences from all over the country. Rahab coaches using good ole southern mannerisms. She teaches it's better to be a tease than a loose cannon.

"Lure them in and then take it away," she advises, using provocative arm and body movements. "Make them pay for it and then dream of it when they catch wind of your scent lingering on their shirts. We don't want fly-by-nighters; we want clients."

Each woman is specially scented in Big Mama's oils and named after the fragrances, Jasmine, Cinnamon, Citron, exotic Ylang-Ylang, and more.

They not only smell good; their bodies and souls are dressed by Lydia. She nurtures them while creating show-stopping outfits. Her designs go from dazzling to gone in the blink of an eye. Lydia literally lays hands on the girls as she measures and speaks wisdom into their spirits. She encourages them not to allow their situations to become their only circumstance.

"You have a savior who's crazy about you, and He desires your heart." Lydia acquaints through familiar hearty laughter and sometimes tears. Quite a few women have accepted the invitation to God's calling. Many continue to dance, prostitute themselves, and do drugs but Lydia doesn't allow that to discourage her. The process of salvation to sanctification is a personal journey as well as the job of the Holy Spirit. She holds Bible studies with the girls from their basement studios. At one point, Jeremy was losing them left and right. He noticed the subtle changes in their demeanor; they were never rowdy in the first place, but they started believing they were too good for the acts they were being paid to perform. Jeremy began nosing around until he discovered the culprit.

He warned Lydia, in not the nicest of terms, "While you have the privilege of working with me, I suggest you keep your religious beliefs to yourself..."

There were tears that day, followed by a fight. Jeremy cleaned the floor with Silas, but Silas gave him a run for his money. It was a fair fight. No weapons were involved. Jeremy burst into laughter afterward as he entertained thoughts of breaking one of Silas' arms or a leg for reputation's sake. Instead, he lowered a hand to lift him up. Silas' relationship with Lydia was commendable and to fight for her, respected.

"I gotta give it to you, Si; you've got balls." Silas took Jeremy's hand and got up from the floor. "And not a bad left hook either. No match for these bullets, of course." Jeremy flexed his muscles. "You need to hit the gym with ya boy."

Silas found no humor in the situation, but he did get the senses knocked into him.

"I don't know about all that, but I could've tried talking to you instead of denting ya jaw like that," Silas responded, pointing to Jeremy's busted face.

They both laughed.

"I respect ya gangsta," Jeremy stated, inwardly knowing that if he killed him, he'd have to take out the entire Auguste/Williams clan. He was wrong in his approach with Lydia, but he ran a strip club not a synagogue.

Jeremy decided to overlook Lydia's behavior. Her designs are sought-after in the industry, and his girls get first dibs. She says that God grants her visions. Her costumes aren't merely beautiful; they're breathtaking and meticulously designed. Keeping Lydia around is good business, but it was against Jeremy's better judgment to allow her and Silas to return to the basement apartment when they moved back to the Bronx.

I AM RAHAB

Though Rahab doesn't dance anymore, her reputation and work with the Vixens draw a crowd that's filled with average citizens and celebrities alike. Her popularity, especially amongst men, still doesn't sit well with Jeremy. She's a superstar in her own right, but to Jeremy, she's property.

JC MILLER

GAME CHANGER

"I need you to do this for the business," Jeremy loudly stated, urging Rahab to return to the stage.

"But you promised I would never have to strip again," she whined, growing tired of his business-first attitude.

"We can't pass up this opportunity. With this kind of money, we can retire from *Vixens* for life," he proclaimed, lowering his voice and running his free hand through her hair. This type of request needed sugarcoating. "We can move to that big house on the Island you've been eying," he slyly baited her. On Sundays, they get away from the city and imagine a quieter life in the burbs.

"Jeri, I don't wanna strip. You promised."

It was a Saturday evening, and Rahab and Jeremy had just finished an overdue romantic dinner at *Sammy's Fish Box* in City Island. Jeremy had been acting strangely all day, warming Rahab up with fake kisses and cold hugs, but on the ride home while stuck in Pelham Parkway traffic, he spilled the beans.

Jeremy and his *real* business partner, Mark Canaan, are in the midst of the most significant deal they've made to date. The usual suspects are up for grabs: real estate, drugs, sex, and gambling. The men put together a group of elite investors that includes the Jewish mafia, drug cartels, political officials, and professionals alike. Every type of gruesome creature crawled from up under a rug and attached themselves to Canaan's casino deal that was orchestrated by Jeremy Cole, Canaan's young apprentice. The project has been in the makings for three years and finally approaching reality. So, Canaan arranged a celebration at Vixens in Harlem. All of the game changers will be in attendance, and everything needs to run smoothly. Canaan, never fond of Jeremy's relationship with Rahab, suggested her act as a grand finale. Not only was she the best woman for the job, Canaan knew that if she agreed, Jeremy's feelings toward her would change.

"Never allow a chick to mess with your money, J-boy; that's messy. You know better than this," Canaan reminds Jeremy every chance he gets.

Canaan raised Jeremy from a kid beating the streets of Brooklyn and saved him once or twice from *juvie* charges. Now, Jeremy oversees everything for him from million-dollar drug deals to dime bags. Canaan trusts Jeremy like a son. He has no doubts about his capabilities. As usual, he expects everything to go seamlessly, and with Voodoo Doll dancing, not only will the minds of any naysayers change, but her status with Jeremy will as well. For Canaan, it's a win/win situation.

***

"I know what I said!" Jeremy stated, raising his voice as he and Rahab entered their penthouse apartment. "But this is the opportunity of a lifetime," he repeated, bringing his tone down and tossing his gray chinchilla fur coat on the sofa. "I'm asking you nicely to reconsider our prior arrangement and do this for our future." He brings his point home by lifting Rahab's hand and kissing her ringless finger. He knew she wanted to get married.

Rahab loves Jeremy, but not as a woman seeking marriage should. They're good together. He makes her feel secure, and security is something she's lacked over the years. All Rahab wants is the best for her family. Marrying

Jeremy, no matter his downfalls, will secure them for life and finally end the nasty rumors of her being his personal prostitute.

"Money like dis don't grow pon tree. Yah gwine dweet!" Jeremy yelled in full Jamerican accent, growing tired of begging.

Rahab *was* going to do it, but not because Jeremy said so. She'd do it for her future.

"If I dweet!" she mockingly yelled back, removing her matching chinchilla fur and *red bottom* stilettos. "Then will we get married?" she questioned, tilting her head.

She needed to know if their relationship was merely business or could they have a future. Jeremy once mentioned that he wanted a *Bonnie* to his *Clyde,* and Rahab felt she'd met the credentials long ago, but even *Bonnie and Clyde* had more going for them than just money. So, she issued an ultimatum.

"If I dance, we get married...like right after. Nothing fancy, just you, me, and the Justice of the Peace. I'm not playing, Jeri. If you can't commit to that, then what am I doing here?" she asked him and herself inwardly. Lydia's preaching was starting to get to her.

Jeremy uprooted Rahab from the floor, and she wrapped her legs around his waist. He didn't want to discuss marriage nor her dancing any further.

"We'll have enough money to do whatever your heart desires, doll face. If marriage is it, den we dweet," he laughingly answered to her delight, then carried her into their bedroom.

POLE LIFE

Scanning the rowdy audience, Rahab stumbles upon Jeremy's face, grimaced with resentment. It is obvious that he's angry. Her heart races.

What have I done?

"Baby girl, never loves a man dat tinks he's better den you, and never loves a man dat can't love you lak he loves himself. Ain't nothin' worse den dat type of ownership." Her Big Mama's pearls of wisdom cultivate her mind. She can feel Lotti's presence ushering her to leave.

"Dat one's too smooth to hold on to, and he's too fine to waste any'mo of ya time."

Rahab freezes. Her eyes frantically dot the room. *I'm bugging.* She can hear Big Mama's voice clearly over the sound of howling men.

"...and why is ya boobies hanging out lak dis, chile?" A cold breeze runs across Rahab's chest.

The spotlight dims into darkness as Rahab rushes off the stage feeling she's become the accusation of harlot bestowed upon her. She's never done anything this pornographic before. The tears burning her eyes compel her to cry.

"Thanks," she half-heartedly responds as a stagehand offers her a robe and compliments her act. Feeling disgusted with herself, she hands him the wad of money from her performance then runs off before he can thank her.

Rahab's performance initially planned as revenge feels a lot like damnation. She can't erase the thought that she's just a high-priced hoe. She walks swiftly through the corridor leading to her office, leaving howls for more

Voodoo Doll behind. *These are his so-called business partners.* She bursts through the office door.

Angry with Jeremy, Rahab's performance conveyed her dismay. They had three weeks before the grand celebration to prepare for marriage and Jeremy wouldn't even cough up the thirty-five-dollar license fee, let alone go to the courthouse to obtain one.

"You know I hate them places," was his excuse every time Rahab asked.

Feeling rejected and second-guessing her life with him, she assumed the role of trollop and strayed from her usual class act. She invited all of the strippers back on stage for a show-stopping performance. They were the backdrop to debauchery.

Against purple projected strobe lighting and lightly scented fog, the women performed lewd acts with one another. It was hot and naughty. Rahab moved with sensual grace between each dancer to an older *Prince* song that seemed fitting for her return. Becoming *Darling Nikki,* she took part in each forbidden act, dancing and teasing back and forth between the girls and the hungry men.

For the finale, she laid arched over the stage flushed with adrenaline and reaching for the grabbing men as they filled her hands with money. The promiscuous women crawled around her like lionesses coming in for supper. They licked and clawed at her body as the lights dimmed to *Nikki's* cries.

Rahab caught Jeremy's face before the lights went out. It was stern and tight. Instantly, she regretted everything. Everyone there knew she was his girl, but they showed no shame in their reaction. Sitting nearest to Jeremy, Rahab assumed by his long slick ponytail and

I AM RAHAB

Jeremy's accurate description, was the partner he loathed, the one he called an *'Indian-looking mofo'*.

Chief *Dippity-Do* sat smug-faced with his legs crossed, open-crotched. He seemed uncomfortable as he wasn't whistling and howling like the other men. That riled Jeremy more so than the whistling and grunting. Rahab had ticked him off, and she knew it, maybe even past redemption. His temples throbbed with anger as she became every man's fantasy.

Once in the seclusion of her office, Rahab allows herself to fall apart. She tosses herself into a swivel chair facing a vanity table and gathers the white robe tightly under her chin. *Life keeps dishing me one bad hand after the other.* She wants desperately to *fold* but considers her family if she *withdraws* from the game. *Jeremy would make life a living hell.*

Ever since Minton's resurfacing and demise, almost everyone in the family seems to be getting along well. It was as if he was the missing key allotting them the permission they needed to live. They're all happier now.

Puah is still sober, and she and Mr. Jenkins cling to Charlotte. Silas works at a loading dock at night, and when he's not assisting Mr. Jenkins with Jeremy's building, he aids Pastor Paul with a street ministry they started. Lydia works effortlessly designing costumes from her shop and witnessing to young women. Then, there's Gomer. She was doing so well, but sometime after Minton's death and the birth of her second child, she abruptly left home and started running the streets again. Rahab convinced Jeremy to allow her to dance at the club as opposed to her being God-knows-where. Gomer doesn't live with the family, so her whereabouts during the day is still a mystery, but she always shows up for work. Every so often, Hosea pops up and takes her back, but like a wild horse, she runs.

Rahab considers her own life, caught in the dilemma of wanting to protect and provide for her family, and just wanting freedom. She longs for the bayou.

Lydia thinks leaving Jeremy and starting over will be easy; it wouldn't be. He's vindictive. As successful as Lydia is now is how broke she'll be if I leave him. Most of Lydia's contracts come from Jeremy's influence. *All it would take is a few phone calls to end her career and then what? We all end up homeless? Jeremy would rather see me starve than happy without him. Senior was right; what am I doing here?*

Like everyone else, Minton warned Rahab about Jeremy. Through awkward shuttered speech and too many apologies, he conveyed his sincere feelings.

"Rah, I know I ain't been much of a father figure to you. But here I am on my deathbed with nothing to hide or anything to lie about. I want to apologize to you," he said tearfully.

Rahab sat in a chair near his bed, hollowed in expression. She held her head low. She couldn't look at him. His presence somehow made her feel shameful, but in his weakness she sensed peace.

"Rah," Minton expressed through tearful moaning. "I was sicker then than I am now. Believe me when I say I'm sorry. I should have never treated you as I did. I don't deserve your kindness nor forgiveness, but I want to say that..." He bowed his head and tears fell into his chest. Rahab looked up and took his thin hand as he struggled to stop coughing. Her touch only escalated his wailing. "I want to say...I love you. I do. You're my daughter just as much as Go-Go and Cookie. I was a horrible father, and this is my just reward. I want what's best for you." Rahab allowed her head to fall to his side and he patted it gently. "This guy, Jeremy, is no good for you." She moaned and shook her head. "You're beautiful. You're talented. You can do anything you set out to do. He's holding you back. He's robbing you of time and youth," Minton insisted. "Baby girl, find your freedom. Know that the same God in Heaven that loves a bum like me loves you too. Money is fleeting, your family and the love that we have for one another, that never dies. Honor love. Free yourself to be God's love."

Minton's words, easy on the ears, reminded Rahab of Pastor Josh and she cried. She cried for those they'd forgotten, conveniently left behind. She didn't know what became of her bayou family and, as far as she knew, Mags was still waiting for death in the asylum. After the doctors told Puah that Mags' acute schizophrenic psychosis was chronic, and she would basically never change, the administrator asked, "Shall we list you as a primary contact if ever she's sick, hurt, or passes?"

"No," Puah related. "She's already dead." They all turned their backs on Mags.

"You'll be aight, Rah. You got dat good bayou blood," Minton continued in a Creole accent, trying to soothe Rahab of guilt and pain. "You strong like ya maw-maw. You're resourceful and most importantly, loyal."

In the short time they spent together, Rahab kindled a liking toward Minton and finally got to know the man Puah fell in love with. She permitted herself to forgive him. He possessed an inner peace she found attractive; a peace that opened her heart to the idea of a Creator who loved her. It's been a year since Minton's death, and although no closer to an understanding of his faith, Rahab is still open to debate. A debate that often leaves her wondering if God remembers that she exists at all.

I AM RAHAB

THE PROPOSITION

Rahab sits in her office desperately longing for Jeremy to rescue her from her thoughts. Inwardly she knows that Minton was right in his conclusions of him, but fear of the unknown cripples her. She's upset with Jeremy, but he's her stability. And, not knowing if they still have a relationship after her performance is killing her.

Instead of being Rahab's *white knight*, as he once professed, Jeremy cowardly sends Mark Canaan in to speak with her.

"Rah, darling! Your act was a hit. I feel like I need a shower," Canaan rants, barging into her office.

Why knock? Rahab quickly wipes her tears away.

They stare at each other through the vanity mirror as he massages her shoulders. An unsettled feeling washes over her. *He's a wolf in GQ clothing.*

"Listen, we have another favor to ask of you."

Here we go! I should have known; it's back to pole life.

"We have a doctor friend out there who, as we speak, is writing a check for an extreme amount of money toward...let's say the opportunity to meet you." He smiles at the revelation, showing all of his teeth, looking sly as a fox in his silver suit.

Canaan is an older Jewish gentleman if you can call him gentleman at all. He's the playboy type. He surrounds himself with beautiful women but attaches himself to none. A gold ring sits on every stubby finger, and a signature toupee flops upon his head. You can't tell him he's not a *playa,* and with the amount of money and power he possesses, you'd second guess yourself in correcting him.

"What are you saying?" Rahab asks, aware that Canaan's doctor friend doesn't want her vitals.

"J-boy has done the calculations. If you oblige to Dr. John's request, we'll supersede our original projected investment by a substantial amount. So, you see, in the end, you'll be helping the team," he lies.

The real deal is, if she takes the job, she's history.

"Are you asking me to sleep with him?" Rahab yells, standing to her feet. Canaan's *stubby finger* massage is irking her nerves. "Where's Jeri? I know he didn't co-sign to this mess."

"There's over a million dollars at risk, not counting the millions we'll lose from other investors if the doctor pulls out," he adds, now stern-faced. "I know that this is a...compromising position for you, so, I'm willing to cut you in on the deal. You're a professional." He paces the small room as he speaks as if convincing himself. "Look, Rah, you and J-boy have done incredible things with the strip clubs. We're looking to do even more with the casino. The fact is, we need team players."

Rahab's head spins from the chiseling of her heart. *How could Jeri set me up like this?* She does not want a piece of the action. To make an honest name for herself is all she wanted, but Rahab the Harlot seems to be the only name that sticks. Canaan continues filling her in on the particulars, but she's gone deaf.

Then she hears him say, "These men we're trying to impress are heavy hitters." Rahab stares at him in disbelief. *I don't care about heavy hitters.* She sucks her teeth. *Let's say these ballers want next with Voodoo Doll. Would Jeri turn his back and let them run a train on me, the team player?* Rahab's pulse races, as the idea infuriates her.

"Okay, I'll do it!" she blurts, to his and her surprise.

A definite YES resonates inside of her to Eric B. and Rakim's "Paid in Full." *To hell with Jeri. I'ma make this cheddar and bounce.*

"Ookay, yeah! That's a girl. Now you're rolling with the big dogs," Canaan excitedly projects, awkwardly *fist pumping* the air.

"But! I want my cut upfront," she reveals, interrupting his one-man celebration. Her hands arch her hips and the weight of her body shifts to one side as her mouth twists in serious attitude. *Ain't nobody getting over on me no more tonight. Fool me once...*Rahab stares Canaan down.

"Now? You want your cut now?" A sense of seriousness covers his tight white face, and his thin lips draw into a pucker.

Yeah, punk! That's right, that's what I said. Rahab doesn't flinch.

"Okay, Miss Rahab," Canaan coldly states, pulling a stack of one-hundred-dollar bills wrapped in a $10,000 currency strap out of his jacket pocket. "I'll give you half now, and the remainder upon completion." He tears the wrapper and counts out a set amount. He came prepared.

Nuh-uh, come again. Rahab counts along with him and shakes her head to express her disagreement. She shifts her weight to her other side. Canaan clears his throat and adds more to his initial count.

"All hail the mighty dollar," Rahab mockingly states, grabbing the entire amount from his hands.

"I must say, this is a disappointment. We're like family," Canaan insists, waving his empty hands back and forth between them. She tightens her twisted lips. "I'm not pleased over this display of mistrust, and I know J-boy WILL NOT be pleased either," he adds, using Jeremy's name as a scare tactic.

Rahab arches an eyebrow. "Jeri, won't be pleased? *I'm* not pleased. Will any of you be doing this? Team players? No!" she angrily yells, digging her long, polished fingernail into his tailored suit covered chest.

"Calm down. Let's be professional," Canaan insists, lightly slapping her finger from his chest.

"Professional? This is not my profession, Mark!" *I'm supposed to be Jeri's girl. His Bonnie.* She fans the tightly gripped money in front of Canaan's face while trying to hold back tears.

"No one said you were a prostitute, Voodoo Doll. We're partners here," he mockingly clarifies, fanning the money out of his face.

"Well, this PARTNER expects to see another ten G's before she does anything," Rahab calmly informs him as she tucks the money into the pocket of her robe.

Canaan tilts and nods his head in an acknowledged *touché*. He expected a hard bargain and considered it more of a parting gift. Rahab isn't the average chick. *It's a shame she has to go, but this relationship is getting in the way of business.* He's positive that Jeremy will never look at her the same.

"I'll be back with the money..." he shrugs his shoulders as if to say *no big deal*, "...but I assure you, this mistrust will sever our relationship."

"Snip...snip," Rahab states, mimicking a scissor cutting. "We never had a relationship, and that goes for ya boy too." She notifies the short comical looking man who's already mentally preparing a plan to remove her and her family from under Jeremy's roof.

Canaan awkwardly stares through her for a few seconds longer before departing from the room. His mind is on the future, and Rahab's the past. She slams the door behind him and rests her forehead against the cold, white, painted wood. Her heart races with fear and disappointment.

"When you sleep with dogs, you wake up with fleas," she speaks out loud to herself. *But if all goes well, I'll come out on top.* She tries to push Minton's voice down within herself as she heads for the shower. "If I want peace, I have to buy it myself."

"Peace is in Christ." She hears aloud within herself and chills run up her arms.

JC MILLER

VOODOO DOLL

Rahab can hear his heavy breathing over *Peggy Lee's* "Fever" playing softly in the background. Taking a deep breath herself, she exhales before sashaying slowly toward the pole in the middle of the dimly lit room. *I hope he's at least kind.* Her guest is sitting on a golden throne in front of a circular scarlet satin dressed bed. Before *working the pole,* Rahab detours to a castle muraled wall and discreetly brushes her hand over the eye of a hidden camera, covering it with black electrical tape. *They won't be watching and laughing at me tonight.* She quickly feels for the money she's hidden inside one of the red, thigh-high, stiletto boots she's wearing.

"Welcome to Calvary," she purrs, grabbing hold of the pole and allowing the music to become her stimulus.

The heavyset, blonde-haired, blue-eyed gentleman is mesmerized by her rare beauty. Her velvety black locks shimmering with diamond beads swing against her movements. She slowly removes her costume, one white leather piece at a time. Her signature scent fills the room.

"How may your servant be of service, my king?" Rahab bows gracefully. Unknown to him, she's nervous and silently prays that the Lord will spare her.

The doctor perks up on the throne. His chest expands a few notches, and uncharted territories awaken within him. Her beauty, her smell, her hypnotizing motions transport him back to his frolicking youth. It's been years since he's felt this way. Rahab is more than he hoped for and worth every penny he spent. He'd been with many prostitutes, but none were able to make him feel alive. She hadn't touched him, yet he was preparing to offer her money to leave the city with him.

She's a Voodoo doll alright. He gazes over every inch of her body. Falling under her spell, he pulls out an inhaler.

Rahab moves in closer, noticing his emotional state. *He better not have a heart attack.* She straddles his lap and runs her hands slowly up his chest. His body actually quivers like jelly.

"Voodoo Doll can fix it," she purrs, blowing his blond locks. *At least he has a handsome face.*

"Yes, you can," he agrees in a southern accent, roughly grabbing her derriere. "I haven't felt this way in years, and you smell good enough to eat." His breathing is getting heavier. "I think you done reversed my curse!" He excitedly proclaims before licking her neck like ice cream.

Rahab startles over his sudden eagerness. "Slow down, *Sir Lancelot,*" she encourages, fearing he's going to hurt her.

The doctor raises from the throne, lifting Rahab like a child and carries her to bed. "I can't slow down now. I'm not missing this opportunity." He tosses her on the satin dressed bed. "I haven't been able to do this in over twenty-four years." He reveals his secret, unashamed, tugging at his belt.

Rahab's eyes bulge. *Well, at least it'll be quick.* She lays back and buries her face in the sheets no longer wanting to see him. She can't help but reflect over all the young women she mentored, and Jeremy conned into prostitution; guilt and remorse rise within her. *If you spare me from this lifestyle, I'll serve you.* She promises God, negotiating a foxhole prayer and deeming, belief is better than no hope.

"If Mama Lotti could see me now!" The man laughs, pulling Rahab's reluctant body toward the edge of the bed.

"Wait! What did you say?" Rahab asks, staring the handsome man in his penetrating icy blue eyes. "What was that last thing you said?" She'd been tuning out his rambling.

"Shucks, don't worry none about me. I'm just reveling in this moment. Now come here, girl."

Rahab sits up and they're face to face. "What did you say your name was again?" She is afraid of his answer.

"I don't recall exchanging any formalities, Voodoo Doll. Now, are we going to do this or not?" He pins her between his large arms. "Oh yeah, we are," he declares, roughly pushing her down.

"Canaan said your name is Dr. John. It wouldn't be Dr. John Fontaine, would it?"

His arms stiffen and his mouth falls ajar. *Her face looks familiar.*

"It's the Honorable Judge John Fontaine, Jr., JD…I'm a *Doctor of Law*," he reveals slowly. "Who wants to know?" He's curious now. The scent of lavender awakens his memory, and he instantly hates her.

"Rahab Auguste, de daughter of Puah Marie Auguste and T-John Fontaine, dat's who," she angrily reveals in a Creole drawl, scooting from under his grasp. Her father. Her mother's attacker.

"What kind of poppycock is this?" John Jr. questions, pulling his pants up into the grip of his hand. "I'm sure I have no idea what you're talking about, lil' girl." He frantically eyes the room for hidden cameras, convinced of a set-up.

"Oh, what a tangled web we weave," Rahab laughs, presuming this is his day of reckoning. She rushes around the bed toward him. "I'm your daughter! And you raped my mother. Do you remember that?" She hauls off to smack him, but he defends himself by grabbing her by the arm.

"Now wait just a minute here, little miss doll baby. I didn't rape anyone; your mama was a two-bit whore just like you." *It's been too long to rehash a hotheaded mistake.* He stares Rahab in the face, and her Irish eyes liken to those of his mother's. *She's nothing but a prostitute.* He refuses to believe what his eyes relate. John Jr. shifts his sight past the acquaintanceship of her face and onto her glistening body. He recalls her naughtiness on stage earlier and his body quivers. *I paid good money for this.*

Rahab struggles to maneuver her arm from his clasp. The heat from his stare is burning through her flesh. He releases the grip on his pants, and they drop around his ankles. His yearnings for her are still strong, and he finally feels physically able to perform. *Daughter or not, she's mine.* All too familiar with the panting sound of lust, Rahab tries to escape, but he flings her on the bed.

With every forceful thrust, the past becomes the present and time seems to stop. Screams go unheard over erotic background music as she's pressed down into the scarlet sheets. "I'm your daughter!" Rahab cries, but John Jr. doesn't care. His manhood is thinking for him, and it's overdue in having its way.

His body collapses atop her. His breath is hot, and their cheeks touch as though in a dance not meant to be. "Atta girl," he utters through windedness, stroking her head.

Rahab's skin crawls. At the moment, dying would suit her fine. Thoughts of disgust spark a flame of anger. She closes her eyes and the tears stop running. Her anger is not toward John Jr., she's numb of him. Her anger is toward God. *How could I believe in You again?* She considers the odds of this happening to her twice in a lifetime. *God hates me.* But she can't imagine why.

John Jr.'s sweat rolls down her neck, and she nudges him, wanting out from under his weight. She's glad she taped over the surveillance camera but wishes she could tape over God's eyes as well.

Do you find amusement in ripping me apart? Silas swears it's You who lifted him up in his time of desperation. Lydia swears it's You who answered her cries. Minton swore it was You who cleaned him up and gave him a second chance. Why not me? Am I so wretched that your eyes don't cast upon me? Rahab questions God, growing angrier with each inquiry.

"Why don't you see me!" She screams in frustration, concluding God doesn't care about her, and because of that, she couldn't care less about Him anymore.

"Because you're a dirty little trick," John Jr. smugly answers, now standing and straightening himself. He's elated that Lotti's curse is finally broken. The newly reported information Rahab provided means nothing to him. He's fully contaminated. "And to think I was actually considering asking you to accompany me back to *Gonzales*. I could've used a good *bed warmer*."

His words are dead. Nothing can hurt as much as being hated by God. Rahab rolls over, gathering the red sheet around her body. She feels for her money.

"So, I suppose you feel like a real man now, huh?" She turns her face toward a wall not wanting to look at him but catches her own reflection in a mirror and bows her head.

"Haven't felt this good in years, buttercup," he answers, sensing an urging for a cigar, a shot of vodka, and a long whiz. "Welp, it's been real." He smacks her thigh then awkwardly walks away. His knees bend outward in a bow under his weight, so he limps along slowly.

Rahab quickly turns to face him, amazed by his apathy. *Maybe this is why God doesn't see me because I'm the seed of the devil.* "You're a nasty, son of a...get out!"

John Jr. laughs. "That's right, and when I wake up tomorrow, I'll still be a nasty, might I add rich, son of a...but what will you be? A tramp?"

"Oh, I got ya tramp. Get out!" Rahab yells, getting up from the bed with the sheets wrapped around her and frantically looking for something to throw at him.

He laughs even harder at her ranting. "This has been an interesting turn of events," he airs with his hand on the doorknob. "Maybe now I can have some kids with a real woman."

"Get out!" She shouts again even louder.

As John Jr. leaves laughing, Rahab catches a glimpse of the *Indian looking mofo* and his partner heading into the opposite room with a stripper before the door closes. She falls to her knees and face in surrender. *Death can't come soon enough.* She broods, feeling the bulge of money taped to her thigh and considering it now of no real value.

She wails aloud, "I'm a prostitute and I may as well face it."

In her sulking, she vaguely hears the door open, shut, and gingerly lock. *What now?* Footsteps quietly approach her crouched scarlet sheet-wrapped body. From the corner of her eyes, blurred with tears, she can make out two sets of freshly polished shoes standing near. *Great, a threesome.*

JC MILLER

THE SPIES

Joshua the son of Nun secretly sent two men out of Shittim as spies, saying, "Go, view the land, including Jericho."
Joshua 2:1

He sinks deeper within himself with every piece of her skimpy garment that is strategically removed and discarded. His heart races as he recognizes Rahab through the sultry and edgy routine. Her flowing tresses are no longer the golden sandy color he adored. She's not the bayou tomboy he once reminisced.

Catching his mouth agape, Salmone reminds himself that he's working. Although embarrassed for her, he can't help but stare. Kaleb, his partner, discreetly nudges him, reminding him of his surroundings. They vowed to be accountable for each other and falling into the alluring trap of lust is testing their obedience. Both Christians, they prayed before entering *Vixens* that the Lord would forgive them for what they would see and save them from partaking in any extra activities while on their mission. They'd been in the club for over an hour, and both were successfully managing to see and not see. They watched every act, gazing through the strippers and focusing on the job at hand. But for Salmone, there's something different about this last dancer. Being from Louisiana himself, her introduction caught his attention. His attention piqued more when her bewitching eyes were highlighted on the monitors.

"This next beautiful lady brings the heat all the way from New Orleans! Give it all the way up for the magic of

I AM RAHAB

Miss Voodoo Doll!" the announcer yelled, ushering excitement.

Rahab, disguised in character, owns the entire room but, knowing her as he does, Salmone identifies her almost immediately. Instead of dwelling on the raunchy performance, he observes her more natural movements and quirky gestures sensing that she's feeling some sort of way. Rahab teases and taunts the hungry men, but Salmone notices that she's slightly nervous or uncomfortable by the way she still bites the corner of her bottom lip. She still unintentionally tugs and releases her right ear from time to time in anxiousness. He senses an apparent agitation by the way she curls up her nose at Jeremy Cole, his *supposed* business partner. Her bluish-gray eyes penetrate through Jeremy's cold disposition, and he uncomfortably shifts in his seat.

All of these years I've waited. Salmone recalls his commitment both mentally and physically to her. *This isn't how it's supposed to be, Lord. I waited. This can't be Rah. This isn't my wife.*

Rahab frolics across the sunken platform, lewdly interacting with the other strippers. To make matters worse, she's highlighted on not one but two massive wall monitors. Salmone's temples throb rapidly with anxiousness. Sweat builds above his brow. He's been trying to reconnect with her for about ten years and seated amongst a crowd of drug dealers, strippers, swindlers, and thieves he finds her without trying. Rahab glances his way, and he reddens under her brief scrutiny. Instinctively, he desires to rescue her as in the past; but putting duty first, he watches as she strips away her dignity and erases his dream of a wholesome happily ever after. *She's a stripper and maybe even a prostitute.* Salmone judges, remembering what Canaan announced earlier.

"All extra activities with the ladies are on the house tonight," Canaan exclaimed holding up his glass in merriment and laughing perversely. "Tips are optional, but I'm sure the ladies would appreciate them. Salud!"

To those close to Salmone, his intentions to find and marry Rahab are no secret. He proudly revealed he heard the voice of the Lord tell him that she's his wife. Though many have lost faith in his revelation, he guards his feelings for her.

"Don't forget there's plenty of other fish in the sea. You should date so and so's daughter." Friends constantly urge him to explore his options.

It's not that he has no interest in women, he has plenty of interest; and as exotically attractive as he is, they have interest in him as well. Salmone stands firm in his faith, and no one can hold a candle to the remembrance of Rahab in his heart. Even Pastor Josh questions his son's dedication to a childhood crush. They all loved Rahab dearly, and wish her well, but Salmone's borderline obsessive behavior causes worry.

When Rahab left Louisiana, it was as if Salmone lost a body part. He became disabled in his daily life. He knew her departure was inevitable, and a relationship with her mother was probably for the best, but her absence afflicted him. Solely, he continued in their routine of fishing, setting traps, and climbing the big oak tree that overlooked the bayou. He hadn't noticed the inactivity of his own breathing until Rahab's first letter arrived and he could breathe freely. When she phoned, he listened in silence, absorbing her conversation and laughter. He relished in the thought that she missed him, but as time passed his absence turned into contentment. She settled into a relationship with her new family; she even mentioned a new friend. In teenaged jealousy, Salmone conjured up a friend of his own to flaunt. He pretended the new girl in town and baseball games were more important than listening to Rahab's many adventures in the big city. By the time she and her family moved in with Mags and Richard, their conversations were reduced to holiday and birthday calls then answering machines, and, finally, "Dong, dong, dong! This line has been disconnected or is out of service..." Salmone never imagined complete abandonment. They haven't spoken in nearly ten years.

With time, he's learned to live again. Like an amputee, Salmone manages to maneuver without the missing part, but the longing never ceased. He reminds himself daily that three things will last forever: faith, hope, and love and, for him, the three have never wavered.

Angry with the world after Richard's death, Rahab couldn't find it in her heart to reach out to Salmone for comfort as she used to. She told herself that he lived a *grand ole holy life* and she was too dirty for his righteousness. She thought of him often throughout the years and treasures the memories, but she's changed, and the past is the past. The problem with that notion is, no man can *hold a candle* to him. Even as children, he showered her with love and respect. *The last great romantic. Maybe chivalry is dead?*

JC MILLER

LIGHTS OUT

"Tsk, look at these whack negroids," Jeremy directs to his table pointing toward Kaleb and Salmone. The pair is awkwardly following behind Jazmine, the club's hottest vixen, as she leads them to the Champagne Room. "That's too much for you, Chief Yellowfoot!" he teases Salmone, insisting he's *Native American.*

Salmone ignores the taunting, trying to remain as stone-faced as Kaleb. Kaleb is the senior partner, and although he does have a great poker face, he can't help but feel a tad bit uneasy about Salmone's hastened decision to deter from their original plan and locate Rahab.

During the performance, Salmone quickly whispered to Kaleb, "That's her," and Kaleb instinctively knew who "*her*" was. She's the mystery woman Salmone's been looking for since he arrived in the city, the reason he became a cop.

Seeing Rahab has ruffled Salmone's feathers, and Kaleb can sense him drifting out of cover. For a moment, he considers ending the undercover operation but decides against it because they haven't secured enough evidence.

"She can help us," Salmone states over loud music as they follow Jazmine through the crowded narrow hall toward the staircase. He's visibly sweating.

Strippers are coaxing men back and forth and in and out of every nook and cranny of the building. There's an actual weight of sin consuming the space, and its heaviness bares down on Salmone like a thick fog. His breathing is slightly exaggerated, but he continues to trudge up the dim stairway.

I AM RAHAB

"I have to find her, Leb," Salmone insists, taking a handkerchief to his forehead.

"She's on their side, bro."

"She's not. I know her, trust me."

"You knew her; you don't know her anymore. She's Jeri's girl," Kaleb whispers. "You heard what the Latinos said."

"I've waited all these years. I gotta find out."

"And how do you suppose we handle this little situation?" Kaleb asks, referring to Jazmine. He smiles and winks at her as she turns to make sure they're keeping up. Kaleb licks his lips, pretending to be *bout it, bout it*. She takes his hand and leads him to a closed door. They've reached the top floor.

"If God is for us," Salmone whispers, having no clue. Kaleb exhales, nodding in agreement.

The small area seems clear. Only two rooms occupy the floor. They haven't spotted Rahab, but they both know she's up there. The Champagne and Throne Rooms are the most expensive in the club. Salmone assumed the hottest commodities wouldn't be in any less than the best when he propositioned Jazmine. He and Kaleb overheard the Latinos gossiping about Jeremy selling his lady to the highest bidder and on impulse Salmone approached Jazmine before she left with Canaan.

"Eh, he looks…sorta fun," Salmone said in a condescending voice, grabbing her arm. "But I hear a threesome is wassup." Jazmine smiled, thinking he was cute and whispered something in Canaan's ear before gesturing the partners to follow her. Because of Jeremy and Salmone's love/hate relationship, he and Kaleb were not invited to the private bidding for Rahab. Jeremy would rather Rahab be with anyone other than Salmone, but little does he know everyone now considers her up for grabs.

Just as Jazmine turns the knob to the Champagne Room door, John Jr. rushes out of the room behind them laughing. Rahab is launching insults at him. In a brief moment of awkwardness, they all pause making eye contact before the door shuts.

"She's a feisty one," John Jr. snorts. "I would definitely suggest her, gentlemen," he states, continuing his wrath.

"Is that Voodoo Doll?" Salmone asks.

"Yup, that's that spitfire," he reveals as he sets his intentions on Jazmine. He wonders if his luck was a passing thing or if Lotti's haunting curse has finally been broken. *This could be my luckiest night since college.*

Taking advantage of John Jr.'s perverted opening, Kaleb advances toward the Throne Room ushering Salmone, who seems frozen, to follow.

"Papi, what's up? I got you. You don't wanna go there," Jazmine contends, partly for herself and partly for her mentor.

"I got a million reasons why you should let them go, my little señorita," John Jr. brags, limping into the Champagne Room and forcing Jazmine to enter with the mass of his weight. The door closes behind them.

"We have to make this quick," Kaleb whispers. "We have company." He quickly motions toward a camera monitoring the floor. Salmone silently agrees, mindfully opening the door.

"*Juicy Fruit*" by *Mtume* fills the space with *Sophistifunk*. Salmone and Kaleb glide across the room as not to alert Rahab. Depleted by turmoil, she doesn't move from the floor.

I AM RAHAB

"Rah?" Salmone calls, reassuring her identity in his disbelief.

Rahab slightly turns her head eyeing their polished shoes, then slowly moves up to their linen pants and broad shoulders with opened jackets. *Who dares to call me Rah?* She wonders, feeling annoyed. She was in character as Voodoo Doll.

"Are you hurt?" Salmone questions, extending his hand. He can see the fire in her eyes blazing and gathers she doesn't recognize him. He's the last person on earth she'd expect here. "Rahab, it's me, Sal." He stoops, giving her a better view of himself in the ambered lighting.

The name alone sends a jolting shock throughout her body. A glorious light appears to illuminate the room in a halo above his head.

"Sal?" She queries, trembling with electricity.

Hearing her voice removes any negative feelings he had from the racy performance earlier. She's Rah from the bayou. They grew up together. She's the girl who played hard like a boy. The girl he arm-wrestled but let win just to watch her cheeks sink into deep dimples as she gloated in circles around him.

"It's okay, Rah; I'm here now," Salmone says, making sure that the sheet draped loosely under her arms is adequately tucked as she attempts to stand.

"Sal?" she asks again, confused. She recollects his gentle and caring hand. *But he's the Indian looking mofo. How can this be?* She stares at him like he has two heads, then rubs her eyes seeking clarity. *No way...God, is this you?*

"I got you," Salmone reassures.

At that moment, all is well in the world that holds Rahab hostage. A wailing floods the room as God's love is justified in Salmone Joshua Abrams. Hate melts into hope and arms wrap around each other like the roots of an old tree. The sweet scent of lavender and rosemary drifting from her hair smells like home. The hardened heaviness on his chest loosens like breaking chains. His cheeks tighten and burn as he tries to fight back tears.

Kaleb can feel the choke of emotions in his own throat. *She wasn't imaginary after all.* He shakes his head in amazement, walking toward the window to grant them a little space. *How are we going to get out of this mess? I hope this little reunion is worth the years of sacrifice.* He worries, feeling their cover is blown if Rahab doesn't cooperate. Glancing back at the couple, he senses the value in their relationship and chokes up again. The only time he's heard a woman cry over a man in this way was when his mother put his father to rest. *We'll need a distraction to get out of here without being questioned.* He observes a fire escape adjacent to the room's window.

"I hate to break up this happy reunion, but time is not on our side," Kaleb reminds Salmone of their duty.

Salmone hates to pull away from Rahab, but Kaleb is right. They need to get out before Jeremy catches wind of their disloyalty.

"Ahem. Rah, we have to go," Salmone states, clearing the crack in his voice. Rahab doesn't respond. Her face is buried in his chest. Her tears are soaking his shirt, and she's clawing at his tailored suit like she's trying to strip back years lost between them. Salmone's speaking, but she doesn't hear words. He gently palms her face and tilts her head. She can't control her sobbing. His heart melts, and he decides to whisk her away in rescue.

Examining the ground level of the alley below and speaking into a *wire* taped under his suit. Kaleb yells,

"Lights out! Alleyway on the right side of the building nearest *147th Street*."

Club Vixen and the surrounding area are suddenly covered in darkness. A collective gasp is heard throughout the building, followed by a quaking silence. Salmone lifts Rahab from her feet and heads toward the window. The silence of darkness and the gust of crisp winter wind coming in through the opened window alerts her. She's familiar with the evil that lurks in dark places. The men downstairs, although alarmed, are most likely gathering their belongings and quickly and quietly filing out. Her only thoughts now are saving Salmone from Jeremy.

"Wait!" Her loud command startles Salmone before he maneuvers a leg through the window onto the fire escape. "What are you doing?" She's not sure of his plan, but she's confident that they should include avoiding Jeremy. She frees herself from Salmone's comforting arms. Kaleb, who was unlocking the door rushes over to join the escape party.

"We need to get up out of here right now," he advises.

"Follow me," Rahab urges, climbing through the window first before they can speak or stop her.

She's acquainted with the ins and outs of the building. To climb down would place them directly in Jeremy's lap, and knowing him as she does, she's sure that he and Canaan are heading to the office to retrieve any money and drugs. When they're done, they'll leave through the emergency door which exits into the alleyway directly below them. Rahab cautiously leads the spies to the roof.

"They're doing some construction on this building and the vacant one next door." She stands by the ledge awaiting both men to reach the tarred landing. "We can cross over to *148th Street* from here and hopefully avoid being seen by anyone," she explains, adjusting the jacket Salmone places over her shoulders.

Kaleb quickly reiterates the change in plans into the wire as they scatter across the rooftop. Rahab gathers Salmone's jacket underneath her chin, inhaling the scent of a boy turned man as she tries to avoid the assault of the December wind ripping through the satin sheet wrapped around her. Salmone grabs her hand, and together they race through the starry lit night toward the opposite end of the roof. Rahab directs them to the scaffolding connecting a vacant building; they cross over. With each step, her heart pounds with fear.

Is this You, God finally showing up in my life, or am I putting everyone I love in jeopardy? She tries to block out thoughts of Jeremy killing Salmone.

The men lead climbing down the next set of fire escapes of the adjoining four-story building exiting into a courtyard. Rahab cautiously follows behind them, feeling for every iron step with the tip of her stiletto boots. *It would be my luck to fall to my death.* She is careful not to hang a heel, deeming nothing good lasts for her. Nervous, she pauses briefly to catch her breath. She closes her eyes, pressing her forehead against the cold iron bars and cries out quietly in her heart. *Lord, I'm sorry for questioning You earlier. I know that I'm supposed to put my trust in You, but this is all new to me. I want to believe more than anything that You're here with us. I just need to feel your presence. I'm afraid. Please get us to safety. We need You.*

Salmone, noticing Rahab has stalled coming down the ladder rushes back up and covers her with his body.

"God will not fail us nor forsake us," he slowly utters in a calm, reassuring voice, guiding her every step.

Once on the ground, the men quickly lead Rahab into the back of an awaiting van and the doors shut behind them. As they are whisked away through the darkened roads, the street lights return one block at a time, leading them toward Harlem River Drive.

Salmone embraces Rahab. She trembles in his arms.

"Thank you, Lord. Thank you, Father."

JC MILLER

BEHIND THE WALL

I AM RAHAB

INFORMER

For the past year and a half, Salmone and Kaleb have been working undercover with *NYPD*'s drug trafficking unit tracking Canaan's empire. Their manipulated reputations as Solomon *'Solo'* Webster and Kyle *'Ky'* Banneker precede them in the underworld. Becoming partners in Canaan's casino/drug racket came easy. Every man in the club that evening was vested in the deal, including John Jr. The drug lords, under the Jewish Mafia, were merging investments in anticipation of large international cocaine purchases, then reselling the coke for more on the streets to secure revenue toward the casino. The professional businessmen provided legitimacy to the project. The next cocaine shipment date and location were pending, and now that *Solo* and *Ky* are working with Jeremy, they're close to busting the entire ring.

Rahab was tired of Jeremy's abusive treatment, and she was done with him after he and Canaan set her up the way they did. So, she hesitantly agreed to the terms of becoming an informant. Knowing that the duo was being investigated, and her family was possibly in danger bent her arm toward cooperating with the authorities. But trusting Salmone made it all easier. She wore a mini wire device covertly adhered to the inner shaft of her thigh-high boot. She insists, "If anyone can persuade Jeremy to talk, it's me."

She and Jeremy were due to have a heated conversation regarding the prior evening's affairs. "What better timing to coax him into a debate."

Rahab apologizes to the cops for not being able to assist them with the particulars of the business. It never interested her. Not wanting anything to do with the drug scene, she allowed information to slip past her processing. Most evenings, Jeremy sat in his home office running numbers. Some nights, he briefs Canaan over the speakerphone while Rahab massages his stress away. Her duty was to keep him happy not to keep track of his affairs. She fulfills his sexual appetite and assures the strippers brought in substantial capital. Jeremy's motto is, "*make money providing top of the line service*" and meeting the goals he set keeps Rahab busy.

"If asked the right questions, I'm sure I can remember some details," Rahab expresses to Salmone, trying to convince him of her ability to help.

They were parked in the middle of nowhere awaiting an undercover cabbie to arrive with counterfeit money she requested in a trade-off for the twenty thousand she had taped around her thigh. She couldn't face Jeremy without the money, he'd certainly ask about it, and if the surveillance were to go forth, it would be on her terms. So, she made it clear that the money was hers and she wasn't giving it back.

They interrogated her with a million and one questions, and everyone except Salmone seemed to be on board. His heart shared its beat with the informant. His continuance vested in her safety. Nevertheless, Rahab agrees to be *wired*. The undercover cabbie would return her home. A van discreetly parked near Jeremy's building would carry out surveillance and, if needed, rescue.

"Rah, I hate to ask you this, but are you positive this isn't a lovers quarrel, and the minute you two make up, our cover's blown? I got my partners to consider." ...*and my heart.*

"Look, I know it's been a long time but, first off, I would never do that to you."...*I love you.* "Secondly, I swear that I have no romantic feelings left toward Jeremy. All he's brought me is pain. I admit I was captivated by the money, the fame, and even him and how he protected me. But I'm telling you there was never any *real love* involved. My love is for my family and, right now, they're my only concern." She pauses in doubt of revealing her vulnerabilities, "I did something tonight I don't usually do." She lowers her head in awkwardness and unfamiliarity with the newness of exploring her faith in God. "I prayed." She scans the van, glancing over the faces of the four cops cross-examining her every word and movement. Only one matters; the one who holds her affection. "I asked God to save me, and for the first time, I feel like He actually heard and must love me because He sent you. I know I've been stupid, and you have no reason other than our past to trust me, but please believe me when I say...I want out. I'm tired, Sal, I'm tired of fighting." Rahab can't help but cry. It's been an emotional evening for her on top of an overwhelming lifetime. Not to mention, she was just raped by her father. However, she had decided she would be withholding that piece of information.

Salmone knew Rahab's burdens were great. He wished he could erase them. She wears suffering like he wears the *Word of God,* like a shield. His only support is to draw her near. They fit like a lock and key.

"She may be our last hope after tonight," Kaleb interrupts, fearing the compromise of their cover, if not definitely their trust, with Jeremy. The other two cops agree.

"Yeah, but I don't wanna place her in danger because of my...listen, guys, can we have a moment alone?" Salmone asks, now wishing he'd handled the situation differently.

I AM RAHAB

NOT A LITTLE GIRL

"Are you sure about this, Rah? Because I don't feel comfortable with it at all," Salmone expresses once the others have left.

He sighs heavily, sliding his hands over his sleek black hair and resting his head against the headrest. The thought of losing Rahab again unsettles him. She smiles and dries her tears. She's tickled by his concern.

"You're still playing *Super Sal*, aren't you?"

"I guess I am." He doesn't oppose the position of his alter ego.

"Well, you know I've got my own cape now."

"I know," he admits, lifting his head in attention. "I know that you're capable of taking care of yourself. It's just that...it took so long to find you and I...have so many things that I want to share with you and...I don't wanna risk losing you again; I can't."

Rahab turns her face in embarrassment. Salmone's sincerity shames her. *He searched for me? How did I allow myself to get caught up in all of this?* Salmone gently turns her back to acknowledge him. His expression is stern.

"Rah, this is no *coo-yon* we're dealing with. Jeremy is smart and he's dangerous. He'll kill you if he suspects anything."

"I've been with Jeremy for six years; I know what he's capable of." Rahab doesn't mean to confirm Salmone's worries, but she is all too familiar with Jeremy Cole. "Besides," she adds as if on a brighter note. "The surveillance team will be there if anything goes wrong, right?"

"Yeah," he answers. Not sounding convincing at all.

"Listen, Sal; it does my heart well to know that you never forgot me...'cause I never forgot you. But! The truth of the matter is, I've been taking care of myself and my family for a minute now. I'm not a little girl anymore. I don't wanna hurt ya feelings but...I got this." She shrugs her shoulders, attempting to lighten the moment.

"Hmph!" he smirks.

He knows that she's right. *She's a woman.* He fights the urge to allow his curiosity to drift past her neckline. She talks with her hands, and the satin sheet wrapped around her body slightly slips with her every movement. He bites down on his lip to divert his attention and instead focuses on her wavy black hair draped in diamond beads. He twirls a lock around his finger, missing the curly golden sand that once crowned her head.

"Aargh!" Salmone bellows, in frustration. It is a tough situation, but he knows that it is his duty to keep her calm. "May den! Ah guess ah just gotta get used to dis here new you. You in dis here blak hair of yourns, anh," he adds in a Creole drawl.

Rahab snickers then pinches his chin between her fingers as though studying his face. She knows the situation is rough on him; it isn't easy for her either. She stares into his dark brown eyes respecting the fact that he hasn't allowed them to drift below her neckline. She can't say the same for herself. She has no filters.

"Mmm," she moans under her breath, examining his muscular physique in the midst of her dilemma. "Ah guess ah gotta get used to you being dis doggone grown and sexy. Ah mean gaw-lee, boy, you all dat and a bag of chips," she boldly professes, turning on her cunning charm.

I AM RAHAB

The scarlet sheet slips a little further, revealing more cleavage; she wants him to check her out. Instead, childhood awkwardness is rekindled through nervous laughter and then silence. *Be cool. There'll be time for that,* Salmone warns himself. He's been fighting back urges all night.

Rahab strokes Salmone's head like a kitten, and he allows his shoulders to drop and his head to lay back against the headrest. She stares at him in reverie while playing with his hair; it's gathered in a sleek ponytail, and the sides and back are tapered close to his head. She thinks it looks better than his childhood buzzcut that used to stand straight like boar bristles on a wooden hairbrush. The new style suits his chiseled features and kissed long by the sun; reddish-brown skin. *I can see why Jeri thinks he's an Indian,* she muses, considering his strong indigenous Mexican features. She briefly entertains the notion of them becoming an item and quickly writes herself off as unworthy. Salmone isn't the gawky boy she remembers but certainly not the type she accounts herself worthy of nowadays. *He is fine though.* Remembering how weightless she felt in his arms, she traces his jawbone with the back of her finger. The windows start to fog. *Chill, Rah, you trippin. He's straight up five-0 and you...YOU mentor strippers. What's wrong with this picture?*

"The cab is here," someone abruptly announces, knocking on the van window and saving Salmone from awkward flirtation.

"Okay, listen!" Salmone demands, grabbing Rahab's drifting hands. "We're a drug deal away from busting Canaan's enterprise wide open. Jeremy's managed to elude us, but now that we have you, and Kaleb and I are on the inside, we can't lose. I need you to get as much information as you safely can, then get out of there. Act natural and remember, we'll be right there if you need us." He squeezes her hands tighter. "After today I want you to get as far away from Jeremy as possible. Knowing his character, I know that'll be difficult; but if the task force has to raid the building or club, I can't promise that no one will get hurt in the midst of chaos."

"What do you mean?" The situation suddenly becomes real and not merely payback.

Salmone slowly reiterates, "If things get hectic today or beyond and we're unable to communicate, I can't promise that you or any family members who are in the vicinity won't be arrested or hurt in a raid before I can personally assist you. What I'm saying is, it's best that you retrieve the information and get out of the way. Move out of the building and stay away from Jeri."

"Sal, please swear to me by the LORD that I know you serve that you will show kindness to my family," Rahab asks, reconsidering the mission. *No one mentioned raids before.* "Give me your promise that you will protect the lives of my family."

"Rah, this is a dangerous mission. It's not a schoolyard brawl. I can't make any pinky promises."

"So, I have to make sure that we're out of the building after today," she repeats Salmone's directive, feeling panicky. "But...if Jeremy doesn't allow us to move right away...then what? We'll just stay in the basement until I hear otherwise?"

"No! This won't be resolved overnight. It can possibly go on for weeks! There's no way you and your family can all stay in a basement. That's why I don't like this. It's just too risky with you being right up under him." They both sigh.

I AM RAHAB

Granting Rahab an out, Salmone proposes, "You wanna change your mind?" He honestly prefers she back down. Rahab stares at him long and hard and considers all the danger he was placing himself in.

"You know what? I can't hear you right now," she declares, totally determined to keep her family safe. "I WILL get you the information you need today. If Jeremy doesn't allow us to move right away, we'll be in that basement apartment until this thing blows over, period. That means you guys better do your job quickly." Rahab lifts the bottom of the scarlet sheet she is wearing to her mouth and uses her teeth to tear a long strip of material from it. "I'll attach this to our door so there's no mistake which apartment we're in." She tucked the fabric into her boot. "We won't leave until I hear from you, I promise. You have Lydia's cell, right?"

"Yes, we have it." He smirks, impressed with her determination and courageousness.

"And the basement apartment is the second door on the right," she states, reiterating all the details.

"Yes, or the door with the scarlet flag attached to the handle," Salmone jokes to ease her anxiety. She laughs nervously. "Rah, we got it. As long as we're all on the same page and no one betrays us, we'll protect you and your family. *Our lives for your lives.* But! I want you trying to get out of there by tonight. You know what to do; you got this! I just need for you to be safe."

"I will."

"Can I pray for you?"

"Yes, please! Maybe your prayers get through quicker than mine."

Salmone takes her hands. "Father..." He lowers his head, pausing and exhaling before speaking again. "Lord, I humbly come to You bowing in my heart and begging for Your protection over Rahab. You know her story all too well. You are *the author and perfecter of our faith.* No story is any good without YOU finishing it through. Help us to walk in Your will. Help us to trust You and seek You as our refuge and strength. Shine Your presence upon Rah and strengthen her in the power of Your might. Dress her in Your armor so that she might stand firm against the schemes of the enemy. Please..." he pleas in a broken tone. "Walk with her, her loved ones, and our team in a powerful way. I pray that Rah will come to understand the extent of Your own love for her, that it surpasses all head knowledge. I pray that she, in return, will be filled with the Holy Spirit. In Jesus' mighty name I pray. Be our protection. Amen."

"AMEN!" Rahab affirms. Not an *amen* as she's said many times before, but an AMEN she felt rising in her spirit.

Salmone's tender words burst inside of her like an awakening. A warmness waves through his hands and over her body and light illuminates a dark place within her. Salmone doesn't 't stop his tears, not this time. He doesn't cover up his emotions with *male ego* dramatizations. His love for her runs deeper than his pride, and God's plan for them is greater than them both. He stares into her moist eyes. She seems perplexed.

God, please move within her.

Rahab stares back at him in awe of his beauty, not the outer beauty that he obviously possesses, but his spirit that shines through. She knows that they intertwined in another realm and briefly remembers feeling that way standing in front of the pulpit during Big Mama's funeral.

"I'm still with you," God assures in a firm audible voice.

Rahab's eyes dot around the van searching for His presence. She starts to cry, but there is no time for that. She is empowered for the task at hand.

"Thank you, Sal." She squeezes his strong hands. They feel as if they know hard work and are capable of the reinforcement that she needs.

He senses an inner strength in her hands and kisses them with a blessing. "May the Lord God be with you, Rah."

Another knock is heard on the exterior of the van and Salmone quickly vanishes his stray tears.

"Hey!" She grabs him before he can open the door and pleasantly smiles. "Soon come, we'll be sitting back making *vay yay* and laughing dis here off, ya hear?"

"Yup, we will."

Salmone opens the van door instantly re-establishing his cool. Rahab covers her head with his jacket and exits behind him. She quickly heads for the gypsy cab as told. It is precisely 5:00 am, literally a new day. A brisk wind presses against her body but she mets its rage feeling courageous. The cabbie equips and assists her with the necessary details and gear for the assignment. He pretends not to look as she openly removes the red satin sheet and securely ties it around her neck. Before leaving, she spoke privately with Kaleb insisting that he promises not to allow Salmone to help with the surveillance. The thought of him eavesdropping on her with Jeremy is unsettling. She knows Salmone's character, and after the beautiful prayer they shared, she feels ashamed. There is no telling what she will possibly have to say or do to obtain information. She informs Kaleb that the confrontation will be rough, but unless they hear gunshots, she'll be okay.

When Salmone is reluctant to oblige, Kaleb reminds him of his faith. "The same God who you believed in all these years to bring her back to you...and, might I add, my mind is blown that you actually found her...He's the same God who will protect her and secure your union of marriage as He proclaimed."

I AM RAHAB

THE LAST TIME

"What the heck?" Rahab whispers shocked that her front door is ajar. She gently pushes it further in and carefully creeps inside, searching for any signs of foul play. *Mr. Perfect would never leave the front door open.* Discarded clothing spread along the shiny parquet flooring redirects her attention to the open bedroom door, the reason for Jeremy's carelessness. *This bastard is trying to replace me already.*

A seething holler lounges the back of Rahab's throat as she stands off numbed in utter disbelief. She blinks hard, thinking maybe her eyes deceive her, but the hues of daybreak highlight their nakedness through open blinds. She steadies herself against the door frame. Gomer's legs, moist with deceit, are cocked and wound around Jeremy's waist in faithlessness. She's hardly another woman moaning in sinful pleasure, she's Rahab's sister. Blood of the same mother. Family defiling her bed. Rahab arrived ready to fight, but she didn't expect this wrestle. *Jeri has sunk to a new level of low.* She inwardly collects herself.

"Go-Go! What are you doing?" she bellows, startling them and causing them to scramble. Jeremy instinctively reaches for his pistol. "How could you? Why would you?" Rahab temporarily abandons her mission with the spies. Gomer's betrayal takes precedence.

Jeremy laughs, repositioning himself against the plush white pillows Rahab handpicked herself. His perfectly sculpted body glistens with the mist of wrongdoing. Placing his gun at his side, he lights a cigar and, through short puffs, continues laughing at the sister's awkward dilemma.

Gomer uncomfortably leans back under Jeremy's arm, feeling partly embarrassed but definitely gloating in her achievement. Her jealousy toward Rahab has ripened. She longed for her sister to familiarize herself with the pain of defeat, a feeling to which she's grown accustomed. An arrogant mien smears across her face.

Jeremy hadn't planned the betrayal but wallows in malice. It was only a few minutes ago he arrived home eager to confront Rahab. Instead, he found Gomer awaiting him like a present wrapped in vengeance and lust. He followed her at once *like an ox going to slaughter.*

Gomer, along with a few other strippers at the club that evening, witnessed Rahab's misfortune. Jeremy, drunk with tequila and misery, sold Rahab to the highest bidder. His equally miserable mentor, Canaan, egged him on, conducting the bids like an auctioneer. Gomer immediately plotted the jump on Jeremy before another girl had the notion.

"Get out!" Rahab yells with an older sister's authority. "Get out now."

Gomer hesitates, looking brazen, she points toward the door. "No! I believe it's your turn to leave."

In lieu of the *ultimate smackdown,* Rahab exhales and tugs at the scarlet satin sheet now tied around her neck like a toga. She remembers the cops waiting and listening and rejects her urges to pull Gomer by the hair down the hall and out of the building. *Go-Go can wait.* She intently stares at Jeremy; his laughter stops in her silence. Fire is in her eyes.

"Weh yuh friends?" he calmly asks, straight-faced like he knew a secret.

He's aware that his *so-called* partners, Solo and Ky, were alone with Rahab in the Throne Room. He's also keenly aware that everyone knows she belongs to him. He set the rules regarding her and, no matter what he may or may not have said during the auction, the rules stand. *They crossed the line of brotherhood.*

"You tell me since you know so much," Rahab responds, mumbling under her breath. "I'm outta here."

She exits the room confident that he'll follow. Jeremy's far too inquisitive to leave the matter at that. He jumps out of bed, grabbing his gun and awkwardly hopping into his boxers. He cautiously follows Rahab out of the room, unsure of what she might do. *Hell hath no fury like a woman scorned.*

Rahab storms into the living room with her mind frantically searching for plans of attack. Jeremy and Gomer's betrayal threw her for a loop. Then, suddenly, her focus falls on an oil painting by an urban artist with whom Jeremy was acquainted. She struts across the room and tosses the canvas picture upon the floor, revealing a safe.

"What the hell do you think you're doing?" Jeremey yells, following behind her.

"This *joke* of a relationship is over, and I'm moving out of the jester's house," she issues, satisfied with the delivery of her statement. "And! I'm taking what's mine," she adds, turning the lock as if she knew the combination. She doesn't.

If anything will get Jeremy talking, it's his money. He grabs her by the arm and twists her around. Gomer tiptoes into the living room, wanting a front-row seat to the demise of Rahab's reign.

"Yo, don't touch my money. I ain't even playing." Jeremy thrusts Rahab against the wall and wraps his hand around her throat. His temper, easily escalated, went from zero to one hundred in a matter of seconds.

He aims the gun at her head and carefully observes her body, piecing together her evening. The scarlet satin sheet reminds him of her earlier performance. He scowls in disgust. Rahab humiliated him. The fire that usually burns in her eyes when she's annoyed or angry *looks a lot like hate.* Jeremy takes note of that. *Wait! This red sheet is from the Throne Room...which means she didn't go back to the office during the blackout. Hmm, if she didn't go back to the office, she never parted with the money Canaan gave her.* The bruises on her arms and wrists tell him that the men were rough and he's sorry for that. *Maybe she wasn't with them?* She's still wearing her boots which means *she never took them off! That isn't unusual but the fact that money's missing is.*

"Chaz said he monitored that Indian looking mofo and his boy, Ky, going into your room. What's that all about?" Jeremy squeezes Rahab's neck a little harder and uses the gun to maneuver her head toward facing him.

She can smell alcohol on his breath and reckons *he's going to be nasty, violent, and full of himself.* A situation perfect for spilling the beans.

"You tell me," Rahab relates sarcastically. Jeremy tightens his grip on her throat. She yelps.

Gomer slowly approaches, afraid. "Jeri...please don't kill her," she whispers cowardly.

"Shut di hell up! Wah yuh still doing here?" he barks in patois, waving the gun. "Leave, mon."

Gomer slips out of view but doesn't leave.

"Where were you, and why did it take you so long to get back here?" He continues interrogating. "Weh yuh wid dem pretty boys, anh?" Jeremy tosses Rahab to the floor, sucking through his teeth. She coughs, attempting to regain her breath.

"I wasn't with anyone."

"So where did they go? Better question, why were they there in the first place?"

"What do you mean, why were they there? You sent them! We didn't have a tea party," Rahab responds, getting back up on her feet.

"Mi neva send no one but the doc and that was a test of your loyalty, which you obviously have none. I told Canaan you would never take that money and you made a fool of me!" He pushes her head as hard as he can. She stumbles backward but regains her footing.

"I have no loyalty?" she repeats, pointing at herself. "Your money, your drugs, and your women have always come before me," she rebukes, reversing the accusatory finger. "Don't try to play down what happened last night as my fault. We both know that you and Canaan want me out. You have bigger plans that don't include me and that's aight because Rahab will be okay. I do want my money out of this safe though."

Jeremy half laughs, scratching his goatee with the gun. *Since when did she become about nickels and dimes?* He slowly paces between her and Gomer, both were draped in sheets. He laughs louder considering them both whores and takes a seat nearest Rahab.

"You want YOUR money?" he asks sarcastically.

"Yeah, my money! The money *I* worked for all these years. The money *I earned* training them superstar vixens," Rahab yells, rolling her neck in grand Puah fashion.

"You worked for? You did it all, huh?"

"That's right. Those clubs would be NOTHING without me and you know it. Ya so-called Bonnie. Ya, ride or die. Remember that, bruh?"

Jeremy jumps up abruptly and forcefully grabs and squeezes her face. He aims the gun between her eyes and pushes her against the wall. "Let me tell you something and don't you ever forget it. I'm the head negro in charge. I run this show; everyone else is a pawn. Got that!" he angrily announces, spraying spit upon her face.

Rahab is rattled but not broken. She grimaces in disgust and tightly shuts her eyes, proclaiming to herself *this is the last time!*

Up until that moment she'd forgotten Big Mama's preaching on TIME. *This is the last time I'll allow Jeri Cole to mistreat me. The last time he gets to call me out of my name to my face and, God willing, please, Lord, the last time he robs me of any precious moments I have left on earth.*

With redemptive strength, Rahab opens her eyes and stares Jeremy down past the black steel pressed between her eyes. He squeezes her face a little harder in determined spitefulness and moves the gun under her chin, wanting to see the fire in her eyes.

"I'm...still...in...charge," he confirms, rolling each word slowly off his lips.

"*NOW* you are...because I'm out."

"If you don't shut ya lip, you'll find your way outta here quicker than you think." He pinches her cheeks and lips inward. "Yuh tink yuh run dem gals? I pimp you hoes. I'm the one turning y'all out," he insists, now enraging her. "This dope ring, that's me, Jeri Cole. I run the largest operation in Brooklyn. Don't think all I have is because of ya cheap two-step." He releases her face forcefully and begins to pace, waving the gun. Only a woman can anger a man in a manner in which he feels his manhood is put on display, his cool blown, and his assets out.

I AM RAHAB

"Dis deal going down tomorrow isn't because of you. Mi nuh tink suh," Jeremy rants. "I got over twenty of my *boyz* waiting to *cut rocks* tomorrow. This whole building is gonna be *crack central* and I'm getting rid of all you lazy mooching mofo's." He stops in front of Rahab and stretches out his arms as if displaying the apartment. "You think *all this* is because of you? You're stupider than I give you credit for. I'ma push so much *snow* out of this building all five boroughs will be white by Wednesday. I'm the *micky-ficky* man! Not dat wack Indian mofo, his tired buckethead partner, dat hillbilly doctor, or any of them other suckers you *bonin'*. They all wanna piece of what I got!" Jeremy quickly spins her around by the arm, slamming her down on the chaise lounge. She shrieks.

Gomer runs over to help. "Please, Jeri, don't hurt her," she cries. Gomer isn't as strong as she pretends and always bites off more than she can chew. Jeremy can't stand a weak woman and commences to back-slap her with the gun.

Rahab rushes him from behind. "Don't touch my sister!" She jumps on his back like a lioness as he beats her knuckles with his gun. "Get out of here, Go-Go. Now!" She demands.

Gomer runs out of the apartment into the hallway but doesn't abandon her sister. She's conflicted over staying opposed to getting Silas for help. Either way, Jeremy will kill one or all of them. She peeps back inside just as he flips Rahab off of his back against the wall nearest the door. A little stunned and breathing heavily, Rahab quickly stands resisting defeat. Gomer starts to stick her arm through the door to retrieve her, but Jeremy notices and forcefully slams it. Enraged further, he balls his fist and contacts the side of Rahab's head. He hovers over her, daring her to move. She doesn't. He worries and nudges her with his foot. Satisfied with her grunt he struts toward the living room wall unit.

"It's too early in the got-damn morning for this crap!"

Rahab slowly staggers to her feet. "I'm okay, I got this," she announces, speaking to the cops and Gomer with her eyes fixed on Jeremy. She watches him snort a few lines of coke. "So, this is ya new look?" She's surprised but not really by either *blow*.

He laughs, flexing his muscles and beating his chest. "Mi like thunda. Yuh hear mi but yuh cyaa si. Yuh fear mi, gal?"

"I want what's mine, Jeri!" Rahab insists, ignoring his claim and continuing to aggravate him.

Roaring in anger, he rushes her and reaches inside of her loose thigh-high boot and rips the money from her leg, just missing the wiretap. Rahab gasps in fear and surprise.

"I don't owe you *jackbone*." He balls his fist around the money and pushes it into her face. "But you gon' need me tho. Get outta here. You nothing but a trick." Jeremy opens the door and attempts to push Rahab through it. She begins to fight back pretending to be distraught over the money, she reaches and grabs his arms as he laughs with the cash held high above his head. "Mi love a fighta," he taunts. "Jump for it nah."

"Give me back my money you son-of-a..." Rahab gathers the satin sheet in her hand and jumps for the money like a dog for a bone. Malice toward him fills her spirit. Tears build in her eyes. *What if this was all I had?* "Jeri, give it back to me. I worked for that."

Jeremy smacks her and she falls to the ground. He didn't want to be reminded of what she did. He was trying to strip her of it.

"You're a beast," Rahab cries, patting blood from her lip. The fact that she ever cared for him repulses her.

He laughs in sinister fashion, falling against the wall as he thumbs through the money. "Don't sweat me. It's not becoming of you."

"Pfft. Sweat you? Please, your birth was a misfortune."

"Wow, that was raw for you. I'm a god out here and when that delivery comes, I'll be living like the *Rockefellers*. I don't need this ras clot building or ya burnt down borough. I'm from Brooklyn, baby." He bends down and rubs the money in her face. "But you, on the other hand, what you gonna do, huh? Go try-duh find you a little boyfriend and pimp him for some money? Work the streets like ya floozy sistah?" The flames from Rahab's eyes rise and kiss his face. Jeremy finds her beautiful. "You wanna act like a tramp?" He is still hung up on her performance from earlier. He forcefully kisses her, pushing his weight on top of her.

Rahab scrambles beneath him. *This is not going to happen.* She realizes he no longer has his gun, so she bites down on his lip. Jeremy bellows in agony. She clenches harder, forcing him to stand with her. He drops the money and grabs her by the neck, uttering profanity. Choked out, she releases his lip to breathe.

"I should kill you and spare you from poverty," he whispers in her ear. His lip is throbbing, but her belligerency is what captivated him in the first place.

"You already have," Rahab professes. Tears escape her cold eyes.

He loosens his grip on her throat enough for her to breathe and with the other hand he palms her bosom. Their relationship is over, but the question of *love or lust* arises within him because he's never felt this way for anyone before.

"I've given you everything and this is how you treat me?" Jeremy presses himself against her. "Yuh want fi nothing." He thrusts her around, pinning her against the wall so she can't bite him. He starts to pull up the scarlet sheet.

I'm everything she needs.

"Jeri, please. He raped me. Please, not again. Am I nothing?" Rahab pleas, crying. Her thoughts are on the men listening.

Jeremy releases her, and she slides down the wall. *Raped?* He backs away, bumping into Gomer who had re-entered the apartment.

"You think you know everything, well you don't. I'ma tell you what really happened tonight." Rahab stares up at him and Gomer. Her eyes are dark, her face beginning to reveal her battle with Jeremy. "What you did was introduce me to my biological father, so thank you." She nods in appreciation. "And you know what he did? He raped me. Just like he raped Pu." Jeremy and Gomer both grimace in confusion. "He didn't care how much I screamed." Her cold tone breaks in sadness. "I'm nothing to him just like I'm nothing to you. He raped me. He hurt me. He insulted me, and, then, he invited those guys into the room to finish me off."

Jeremy begins to pace. The pieces are coming together. *She can't be talking about the doc. Her father?* He looks back at Rahab. She seems sincere.

"I was in so much pain and feeling so disgusted that all your partners could do was try to help. One of them said he was going for help, but when the lights went out, they were ghost just like the rest of you money-hungry cowards." Rahab lies to clear Salmone and Kaleb's names and re-establish trust.

Jeremy stops pacing. There's a perception in his eyes that reads he somehow cares, but money trumps affection. "Are you telling me that that fat white *bumbaclot* is ya father? And he put his hands on you and raped you?" Jeremy questions, pointing his finger in her face.

"Did I stutter because who would make this up?" Rahab sarcastically responds, pushing his finger away. "I'm tired of this, and I'm done. It doesn't matter how much you hit me, or kick me, or threaten me anymore because nothing hurts more than what you did last night. I've tried to love you, Jeri, and I've done all I know how to make you happy. But this is how you love me back?"

"I didn't have nothing to do with that," Jeremy declares, visibly upset and wondering if Canaan knew. He starts to pace again. Thoughts flow easier when he's moving.

Canaan has been adamant lately about Jeremy getting rid of Rahab. He calls her, *his weak link*. He knows that Jeremy's feelings for her run deeper than sex and can see that she has more power over him than even she knows. *But how would he know something like this?*

"Did you recognize each other right away?" Jeremy asks, stopping in front of Rahab.

"No, we didn't...not right away. He was acting sort of nervous and was having breathing issues, so we talked for a bit and had a brief introduction. I recognized his name and called him out. He grabbed me thinking the situation was a setup, but when he realized I didn't know anything he switched gears. He got angry and raped me," Rahab answers, extending her hand to see who will help her stand. Gomer offers.

Jeremy covers his face and rubs his temples. He agrees that she's getting too close to him, maybe even under his skin. He stands between the sisters; equally beautiful and equally trouble. *They look nothing alike.* It's evident that Gomer is African American. Her skin is the color of graham crackers, and her thick black hair crowns her head and sweeps her shoulders like bundles of cotton. Rahab, on the other hand, is a mystery. *She's light, bright, and damn near white.* Jeremy remembers seeing her childhood pictures and teasing her, calling her a white girl. Her eyes suddenly sparkle, and he remembers the doctor's.

"What's his name?" he asks, digging for reliable information.

"The Honorable Judge John Fontaine, Jr., JD," she calmly declares in the same manner that her father told her.

"Judge? He's a doctor."

Rahab shrugs her shoulders. "According to him, he's a doctor of law."

Jeremy storms off to his office needing immediate answers from his so-called business partners, but prematurely stops and heads back toward the sisters.

"Get out." He snatches the front door open. He's lost his high, so he's pissed about that, too. Gomer and Rahab quickly shuffle through the opened door. Jeremy grabs Rahab back by the hair. "I want you and your family to remain in this building until I verify your story, understood?"

"Yes."

"Yo. I didn't have anything to do with that," Jeremy reiterates, staring into her glistening eyes. She nods. "Get ya money off the floor and get out of here," he quickly adds before storming off into his office.

JC MILLER

SAFE ARMS

Rahab runs into Puah's arms, and they tightly embrace. She and Gomer had no other choice but to wake her; neither girl had their key for the apartment nor a pocket to place one.

"What happened to my baby?" Puah yells, shocked by Rahab's appearance. An explanation isn't needed. Tears instantly flood her eyes at her daughter's wailing.

Puah sensed something was wrong that night. Neither daughter had responded to her beeps or calls. Then there they stood, wrapped in bedding at her door. One girl is badly beaten, and the other looks guilty as ever. Rahab doesn't have to speak. Puah intuitively knows her pain. She's familiar with that type of cry. There are no words; they simply need each other. She leads her daughter into the bathroom and closes the door behind them.

Steam fills the small room. Their bodies, dripping with sweat, become hidden amidst the fog. Rahab strips herself of the prior evening's attire and flushes the mini wire as advised. She then sits in the tub and cries as her mother attempts to wash away any traces of agony, disgust, regret, and fear. She massages Rahab's shoulders and hums a hymn embedded deep within her until a notion presses upon Rahab's spirit. *All things work together for good for those who love God, to those who are called according to his purpose.* She remembers Pastor Josh trying to explain this to the young and doubting bayou lass that she once was, and just like that it becomes a revelation. Her insides warm, and a chill runs across her arms. *Through it all, God has never left me.*

I AM RAHAB

Rahab shares the prior evening's occurrences with Puah, and by the time she finishes, she's comforting her mother.

JC MILLER

COLUMBO

"Are you okay?" Salmone nervously queries. He was briefed but wants to hear it from her.

Rahab stares long and hard at herself in the foggy bathroom mirror, mulling over the question. Her knuckles are black and blue. Her back hurts. Her top lip is swollen, and her face is bruised on one side from scalp to neck. "I'm good," she concludes. It's been a while since she'd fought back, and that alone is encouraging.

"Are you being truthful or are you sparing my feelings?" Salmone inquires, not sure if he can face the truth himself.

Kaleb respected Rahab's wishes and did not include Salmone in the stakeout. He only stated, *"Yo, it was rough, but ya girl is hardcore. I don't know if you can handle her, bruh."*

"No, really I'm fine. Did the surveillance team get enough information? I was worried about clarity."

"No worries, everything was loud and clear. Listen, I am so proud of you. I hear you handled yourself like that superwoman you told me you are." He feels horrible over the fact that, if she took a licking, there was nothing he could have done. The thought angers him. She was right in having him sit out on the surveillance.

"I tried," Rahab responds, attempting not to cry. Salmone's tone of voice is comforting. "So, when are you coming to arrest Jeri? I wanna get out of here."

"Trust me, I want you out, too, but it's not gonna be that simple. We have to plan carefully. I do have a few quest—"

"What do you mean *plan*? He admitted to selling drugs, prostitution...what else do you need?" Rahab interrupts, feeling anxious. As long as Jeremy is free, she can't live a normal life.

"Yes, and all of that information is incriminating, but we need solid evidence against them if we're gonna put em away. We need a hand-off of currency and drugs."

Rahab sucks her teeth and sighs deeply. "Well, the deal is going down tomorrow; we know that."

"Yes, and thank you for that. It narrows things down a lot, but we still don't know where. We have a—"

"What do you mean, you don't know where? It's here in the building tomorrow."

"We're kinda leaning in that direction as well, but it doesn't make any sense according to his pattern analysis, and he never really clarified so—"

"Sal, please! You must be as tired as I am. Don't get all technical. There is gonna be a large cocaine deal happening here tomorrow, in this building. All you guys need to do is be prepared, and don't mess up everything I stuck my neck out for."

Salmone laughs inwardly. She is still a spitfire.

"Trust and believe, the last thing I want is to mess this up. I need you and your pretty neck," Salmone admits, wishing he'd left the last part out. They're on a recorded line.

Rahab blushes. Not as much as I need you.

"What I'm saying is normally Cole doesn't do business where he resides. So, this concept would be out of his routine and—"

"And? And what?" Rahab yells, frustrated. "Jeremy doesn't do dirt where he lives, that's true. But! There are two new factors to consider. One, Jeri has become a user of his product. I saw him, and that changes his game," she relates, confident of her conclusion. She knows personally how an intelligent, strong man can cripple under the domination of drugs. "Two, I have a feeling that this isn't his residence anymore."

"Why?" Salmone asks, pondering her reasoning. She does know Jeremy best.

"Well...because he slept with my sister in our bed." Rahab is slightly embarrassed, but truth takes precedence over pride. "He never does dirt where he lives, like you said, especially that. In his words, 'it's messy, and a good dog never poops where he sleeps.'"

"Well, you mentioned him using. Maybe he got sloppy? Most men do what they gotta do in the moment."

"Yeah, but nah. Jeri is real anal about his apartment, his belongings, and he's funny about his bed," she states, revealing his germaphobe tendencies and remembering their first time together was in another room in the apartment. *Hmm, maybe this wasn't THEIR first time?* Salmone's cross-examining is causing Rahab to doubt herself. "Anyway, Jeremy Cole does not reside here any longer. I'm sure. That makes it okay to do business. He said that he can't wait to get out of this building, and this burned down borough. He also said he has twenty men in the building waiting to cut rocks. Does that sound like a person not doing dirt where he lives?" Having heard the edited highlighted version of the tape, Salmone can't help but agree. "This building is officially *crack central*, I know it."

"You're quite the *Columbo*, huh? It must be those *Nancy Drew* and *Hardy Boys* mystery books we read growing up."

I AM RAHAB

Rahab chuckles. It hurts to laugh. "Or that *Barnaby Jones* detective show ya maw-maw used to watch. Remember that?" They both laugh in childhood recollection. "Ouch." She bows in pain and covers her mouth.

"No more *Angela Lansbury* for you today, okay," Salmone requests, hearing the pain in her laughter.

"Okay, as long as you guys stop acting like *Barney Fife* over there and get this job done."

"Oh, that's cold."

They laugh, and, for Rahab, laughter hurts so good.

"Listen, Rah, I have to go," Salmone suddenly announces to Kaleb's ushering. "I think Cole is calling. Call me later after you get some rest. Oh, and if anyone else answers, it's okay to talk to them. This line will be monitored 24-7 until you're out of there. You okay?"

"Yes. Please go and be careful."

"Okay, bye. Love you." *Gah, did I say that out loud? You slipping, Abrams.*

"Love you, too," Rahab responds to dead air.

She observes herself in the defogged mirror. *Am I worth all of this?* "God please protect him."

JC MILLER

BAYOU BOY

Puah and Lydia block the front door with their bodies as Silas pulls and bangs on it attempting to leave the apartment. He hasn't been this angry in a long time.

"Let him out! That jerk needs his butt kicked." Gomer instigates over the chaos, still wrapped in white linen. Waking the rest of the family and alerting them to what happened to Rahab was more important to her than washing debauchery off of her body.

"Papi, please no!" Lydia wails. "You're not thinking clearly. Let's all sit and talk it over. Please."

"Get out of my way, Bugs!" Silas yells, deaf to reasoning.

"Over my dead body, Si. Sit down!" Puah demands, following Rahab's orders to stay put. She can't say she agrees, but she would never put any of her children in harm's way.

"Come on, Si; he's not worth it, son." Mr. Jenkins attempts to persuade him with his arms wrapped around Silas's waist.

Unknowing of the unfolding drama, Rahab exits the bathroom wearing Puah's robe. "What's going on?"

Gomer's blameworthy face tells it all. "Don't worry, Rah. Si is going to handle this. That negro needs to know he can't run us over," Gomer informs her while egging Silas on.

Rahab rolls her eyes. *She never ceases to amaze me.* "Silas," she gently calls, taking hold of her brother's tense shoulders. He hesitates to face her.

"What kind of brother am I if I can't protect you?" He hangs his head. "This has gotta stop." He turns to look at

Rahab. The state of her face sends him into a blind rage. He bangs and pulls at the door harder.

"Minton Silas Williams, Jr., God has a plan and a purpose," Rahab loudly declares, silencing the room.

Only Puah is aware of her newly found faith, amongst other things. She notices Rahab's face brightens when she spoke His name. Her heavy burdens lightened at His mention. She's never heard her daughter utter anything about God before, then there He was. Puah was careful with her words and mindful of allowing Rahab to complete her story. Not a fan of Godly conversation, she let her daughter mention His name when otherwise she'd interrupt in disagreement. This time was different. Through unfortunate circumstances, they'd connected. Rahab's soft-spoken words, gentle and sincere, warmed Puah's stubborn heart and had her questioning her beliefs. *Have I missed the mark?*

"*All things are possible to him who believes*, isn't that what you always say?" Rahab reminds Silas. "Please listen. We can't interfere. This is our opportunity to get out of here forever. Allow me to explain *the whole story*." She looks at Gomer then extends her hand. They had shared a tender moment in the elevator coming down from Jeremy's apartment. They didn't speak, so Gomer only knows half the truth. A silent unified agreement of apologies and forgiveness was established through tears. Gomer knew her sister was courageous, but she had never acknowledged her strength. Now she considers her own actions and motives foolish. Hosea would say she "*sowed the wind and reaped the whirlwind.*" Nothing in her life makes sense but being in Rahab's arms at that moment felt real.

It was time for healing, doused in salvation, for a family firmly bound through turmoil. Puah cooked and served a large Sunday's breakfast while the family quietly listened to Rahab's story.

Although ashamed, Rahab left nothing out from the previous evening. Her family knew the consequences of her lifestyle. Many times they turned a blind eye to the truth for comfort at Rahab's expense, and they were sorry.

"I've never felt so belittled and disgusted in my life. I can't even begin to express how I felt. What happened with Paw-Paw shocked me. I was scared, hurt and incredibly sad but this...this was different. It was more like an awakening. I remember thinking, why are you screaming? Aren't you a prostitute? Isn't this what you do?" Rahab disclosed, looking at the hardly touched plates of food on the table that Puah kept nervously replenishing. No one had an appetite but the kids who were eating in the living room and watching cartoons. "Sorry, I know y'all are trying to eat." Rahab apologized to empathic head shakes of excusal. She paused and gagged. Puah's food along with reliving the incident was making her queasy. Tears lined her face as she tried to compose herself.

"Ay, dios mio," Lydia whispered, cupping Rahab's hand and crying herself.

"If it wasn't for the hate building up inside of me, I probably would've thrown up. The crazy thing is, my hate wasn't toward T-John. I hated God, and I was sure He hated me, too," Rahab confessed, fighting back tears. "I prayed, Le-Le, I did. I asked Him to remove me from the situation. I bargained with Him for protection."

Gomer abruptly interrupted in an outburst of sobbing. Rahab's tragedy had hit a raw nerve. Gomer was *the brash, rebellious type* who was *never content to stay at home*. Of course, she had a story. Rahab's situation wasn't uncommon to her; she fought her own battles and privately bottled and shelved them inside herself. The gist of Gomer's running was mostly from God. She ran from His eyes because they dissected and convicted her. They made her feel peeled apart and unworthy of Hosea, the love of her life. It's not that Gomer doesn't want a decent life. *While she desires to do good, evil is present.* No amount of money, drugs, sex, or food can hide her from herself. Hearing Rahab's confession opened her bottles.

Silas got up and started to leave. The crying was too much for him.

"Wait, Si." Rahab quickly wiped her eyes and took his hands. She didn't want him to feel downcast. A celebration was in order. "I THOUGHT God hated me, but He actually loves me more than I love myself," she clarified as tears built in Silas' eyes. "Yes, I was raped. I was humbled. I was forced to ask myself questions that I've been dodging. I wanted to give up on life, love, faith. Everything. The only way God could show me that He loves me, that He exists, and that He's never left my side wasn't by rescuing me. I got myself in that situation. I was too busy trying to fix our lives to listen to Him in the first place. Had He rescued me from that, honestly, I can't say I would've given Him the props He so rightly deserves. God had to show up and physically move me into faith and action. He lifted me when I surrendered. When I was depleted of self. I was searching for an out, and He stepped in and literally opened a window. He physically lifted me from the ground like I was a piece of paper. I felt weightless and small."

Silas dropped to his knees and pressed his face into her lap. He couldn't control his tears. He knew exactly how

Rahab felt and was overwhelmed with gladness that she now believed.

"The Throne Room was dim, but I swear it lit up. He gave me an ultimatum; either I *follow Him* or stay stuck in my mess. I felt a cold wind blow against my body, that's when I truly opened my eyes, and there he stood. The only person God could send besides Big Mama that would make me believe one-hundred percent that He's my God too…you'll never guess who it was."

"Who?" they all asked, except Puah. She'd heard the story and smiled at the recurring light that brightened her daughter's face. *She's fallen in love twice in one evening.* Rahab's light drew Puah in. No *mojo bag* has ever made her feel that way.

"It was Sal," Rahab shrieked, to some of their confusion.

She then went on to explain and re-familiarize them with the Bayou boy turned cop that held her heart. Although angry with Jeremy, they all agreed that waiting in the apartment is the best decision. Most of them trusted in the Lord, and all of them supported one another no matter how hard life hit them. They ate and planned to move.

I AM RAHAB

SCARLET COVERING

"Why the heck is this hanging on the door?" Jeremy yells, walking into the basement apartment uninvited with the strip of the scarlet sheet in his hand.

He's noticeably different. Sweat is rolling from his brow in the middle of December like it's a summer day. He seems unsettled. He could use a fix.

"And how are you this evening?" Puah asks, reminding him of his manners while annoyed by his barging in. *I hope Si stays in the back until he's gone.*

She turns the volume up on the television a notch. Silas had just slipped away to call out on his job. He also wanted to call Pastor Paul for prayer.

"Yeah, yeah. What's this Voodoo crap?" Jeremy repeats, balling up the strip of fabric and tossing it on the ground.

"It's a covering," Mr. Jenkins explains, sensing no one else had an answer.

"I know that; duh! It's a piece of my damn bed sheet, but what the heck is it doing hanging on the door?" He remembered that Rahab was wearing it earlier.

"No, he said it's *a covering*," Lydia reiterates, stepping forward. She and Jeremy are on better speaking terms than the other members of the family. "It's a sign of protection."

"Yeah, to protect us from you," Puah mumbles. She's as angry as she can be and finding it hard to pretend. *He abuses my daughter...treats her like garbage and has the nerve to walk up in here like nothing happened.* Puah shakes her head, pretending to focus on her program.

"Oh, well it's not working cause...heeere's Jeri." He is the only one to laugh at his joke. He sucks his teeth and questions about Rahab's whereabouts. "I got something to make my baby-boo happy. You chumps don't know how to do that." He walks off to find her.

"Hi, Jeri," Charlotte yells from the bathroom as Jeremy walks down the hall. She and Krystal are bathing with the door open.

Charlotte likes Jeremy; he reminds her of Minton, and although Jeremy would never admit it, he enjoys her company as well. The first time Rahab brought her upstairs to their penthouse apartment to visit, Charlotte and Jeremy laid on the floor and watched *The Wiz* in its entirety while Rahab cooked Charlotte's favorite meal, fried chicken with mac and cheese. Jeremy had started out in his home office, but the music and aroma coming from outside the door seemed to call him. He sat on the sofa intrigued by Charlotte. She knew every song by heart and wasn't intimidated by him. She hardly acknowledged his presence.

"I'm sorry, is she disturbing you, babe?" Rahab asked, coming out of the kitchen to check on her.

Stone-faced, Jeremy waved his hand gesturing her to leave. He was okay and didn't want Charlotte disturbed. Mid-way through the movie, as *Nipsey Russell* sang, "*What Would I Do If I Could Feel*," Charlotte invited Jeremy to the floor. He surprisingly accepted and awkwardly crawled beside her. Before long, she had him hypnotized in a sing-along. Not once did he check his pager or think about business.

As a child, Jeremy had an older sister with special needs. When he was six, she died of pneumonia. They used to sit and watch cartoons together, and she too would sing along. Revisiting his past isn't something he typically entertains, but Charlotte reminds him of his sister, and he secretly cares for her. He buys her things and never rejects her tight hugs around his waist. They don't require his involvement. She lays them on thick and quickly retreats. Reciprocated affection isn't necessary. Charlotte speaks her feelings through song and dance and only requests snacks in return.

"Whassup, cutie pie, Cookie," Jeremy cheerfully responds, leaning against the door frame. "Hi, Krystal," he acknowledges Silas and Lydia's daughter as well.

"Hi," Krystal whispers, slightly waving and bashfully bringing her knees up to cover her flat chest. But not Charlotte. She splashes into the water like a dolphin.

"Watch this, Jeri!" She flops around getting water all over the floor. Jeremy and Krystal can't help but laugh.

"Yo, you off the hook for real." He watches the young child swim in the tub like it's an ocean. *Sometimes you have to make your reality appealing.* He smiles, now in a better mood. He loves how her mind works.

"Did you see that?" Charlotte loudly queries, wiping water from her eyes.

"Yup! You did that, girl. Now make sure you clean behind them dolphin ears." He enjoys her giggles before turning to Krystal and asking slyly. "Krystal. Where's ya auntie?"

"She's in our room sleep." Rahab and Gomer laid down for a quick nap over eight hours ago.

"Y'all almost done!" Puah yells from the living room.

"No!" They both answer, giggling.

"Bye. Y'all about to get in trouble," Jeremy declares, walking away.

"Jeri, you got cake?" Charlotte yells after him.

"Nah, I forgot. I'll tell Rah-Rah to get you some," he yells back as he opens the bedroom door.

***

"Get ya tired raggedy bum-bum out of here," Jeremy demands of Gomer, turning on the lights.

"Excuse you," Gomer shouts, rolling her eyes. She was already getting up. She can't believe she slept with the enemy. *Sometimes dreams are best when they're left dreamt.*

"Yeah, you're excused," Jeremy snaps, pretending to hit at her as she walks past. *Nasty freak.* He can't believe he slept with her. *If there was room for reconciliation, it's over now.* He watches Gomer leave the room. He can't help but notice the size of her derriere.

"Leave her alone, Jeri." Rahab slowly sits up. Her body feels like a *Mack truck* hit it. She winces in pain. *What is he doing here with my family?* She wonders how long he's been there as she tries to remain calm.

Jeremy takes a seat on the bed and wipes his brow with his coat sleeve. "Damn, you look bad."

"Yeah? It wasn't the look I was going for either. What is it? Can we move yet?"

He ignores her haste to leave him. "So, you and Go-Go have a catfight over me?" He meows and claws at Rahab's unamused face.

"What the heck was that about, anyway? Y'all seeing each other? Because I know you don't *poop* where you sleep," she mocks.

"Please." He sucks his teeth. "That poop was there when I got home. What ya boyz *B.B.D.* say about dem big butts and smiles?"

"Hmpf, well I hope it was worth it."

"I'm kidding. You know I'm not interested in Go. She was there when I got home. Plus, I was high and mad as hell at you." He stares at Rahab's beaten face. Sorry but not sorry. *She needs to learn some respect. She thinks she can talk to a man any way she wants.* "Why don't you…come upstairs and get dressed. Let's go out for dinner."

"What? Rahab responds with bulging eyes.

Jeremy shocked himself with the statement. He doesn't really want to go anywhere. He kinda just wants to hold her. All day, he's been feeling strange, sort of jittery. He doesn't desire to be alone but doesn't feel like entertaining a stranger either. Rahab knows what he likes. Only she can work the kinks out of his neck. He's nervous and doesn't know why. On the surface, he appears hardcore. His smooth dark chocolate face is unreadable, but the inner man is in constant turmoil. He doesn't fully trust anyone and feels that everyone, somehow, is out to get him.

He killed a man today. It wasn't his first icing, but this time the Grim Reaper clung to him. His scythe taps on Jeremy's shoulder. Why am I feeling like this? It must be her. That's why I'm here instead of home like I should be. She's under my skin like bones.

Rahab's story panned out. Jeremy, Canaan, and their henchmen took John Jr. for a long ride.

"So, tell me about your evening with my girl." Jeremy matter-of-factly spoke with his arm wrapped around John Jr.'s shoulders.

He sat squeezed between Jeri and Canaan in the back of a limo. He thought they were heading to a meeting.

"You know how it is…she teased, I watched. It was an incredible experience. Thank you."

Hearing his *thanks* made Jeremy feel some kind of way.

"Hey, Doc. Did you know our rooms are all monitored and my friend over here isn't happy about what he thinks he saw?" Canaan revealed, pointing to Jeremy.

John Jr. laughed nervously. "We're all adults here, right? I paid good money for a fun evening with Miss Voodoo Doll. So, technically, I'm not obligated to disclose what went on privately between us…adults."

"Hmm, did you learn that in law school? Tell me about Puah?" Jeremy asked. His question met with more nervous laughter.

"Oh, yeah," Canaan added. "Did I mention the microphones we also have placed in the rooms?" He playfully straightened John Jr.'s tie.

"Ahh, no you didn't mention that…tiny, little, significant fact."

"Well, enlighten us about Pu, JUDGE," Jeremy insisted.

"Puah, Pu. That's a good long story. You see. Hmm." He began to sweat through his heather gray suit.

Jeremy used his free hand to unzip the crotch of John Jr.'s pants. John Jr. started to elbow him and Canaan, but the men in front of them stopped him with smirks, showing their guns.

"Now listen here," John Jr. insisted with authority in his tone. "Puah Auguste is a no-good tramp from Gonzales, Louisiana. She and her Voodoo loving momma disrespected my family, and I don't think you gentleman really have anything to do with that."

"Why didn't you tell us you were a judge? Are you hiding any more secrets?" Canaan asked, cleaning his nails with a sharp knife.

The limo stopped in a deserted remote location. John Jr. swallowed hard, feeling his pulse in his throat.

"I have to consider my reputation. My family name...carries a lot of weight," he explained, stalling as Canaan drew invisible circles around his crotch with the knife.

"Doesn't sound like you have a good reputation...rape, incest, drugs. Sounds like a tabloid party." Jeremy opens the car door.

"Listen, whatever you guys want I'll pay it. I'll do whatever you ask."

"Tell us about your partners, Solo and Ky."

"Who?"

Canaan opens John Jr.'s zipper wider with the knife. "I don't see nothing... You guys see anything down there?" They laughed, yelling nah, nada, nothing, zilch.

"I don't recall those names!" John Jr. shouted over their taunting.

"The two guys you sent into the room to finish off your daughter," Jeremy yelled, putting him in a headlock and dragging him out of the car. He was tired of playing games.

"Wait, what? They offed her? I just sent them in for a little fun, that's all. I swear I don't know them guys."

They all laughed at his confusion of terms and continued to drag him across the lot toward the river.

***

"Really, Jeri?" Rahab yells, interrupting his trance. "You sell me to the highest bidder; then you wanna take me out for dinner? What the–"

Jeremy jumps up and starts to leave the room. His mind is cluttered. *I could use some sleep.* He's only had a brief nap in the last twenty-four hours. He stops at the door but doesn't face her.

"Come out; I have something for you."

Rahab's heart races. *Did I push him too far?* She's recalls reading about a massacre where a *drug lord* had an entire family killed execution-style. She searches for Lydia's cell to call Salmone but remembers it's on the living room table. *Stop bugging, Rah; he looks like he's missing a good thang, not going psycho.*

I AM RAHAB

C.R.E.A.M

Rahab leans against the arched entryway watching as Jeremy playfully taunts her family with smart remarks. He's dressed in casual urban gear, *Karl Kani* from top to bottom, which is unusual for him on a Sunday. On Sundays, they dress up and go to the Island or Jersey to shop and eat.

He looks and smells good. They gonna love him in jail.

Jeremy turns around sensing her vacant gaze. *Mmm, she's even beautiful in a raggedy old robe.* "Come sit with ya peeps. I want all you clowns to hear me out."

"You got five minutes, Jeri. You are holding up my show," Puah voices. She can't stand his company any longer, and Krystal and Charlotte are pruning in the bathtub.

Jeremy eyes her then walks over and shuts the television off. Mr. Jenkins grabs Puah's hand. Steam is coming from her ears. No one messes with her television.

"I know you've all grown fond of me and consider me an extension of this...unit." Jeremy paces the room, demanding attention. "However, Rah and I are calling it quits."

Who the heck does he think he is? Puah's face reads. Mr. Jenkins nudges her.

"Because I'm not the beast you all think I am, I hooked MOST of you up in a nice building down—"

"Pffft!" Puah mouths in disbelief.

Jeremy stares her down. Her mouth is starting to irk his nerves. "Like I was saying...the apartment is paid in full for six months. Lydia, you're a businesswoman. You and ya druggie can manage on ya own. Go-Go, hoe, you know what's up." Jeremy pretends to *make it rain* to her rolling eyes and neck.

"Hold up," Rahab interrupts, standing. "You mean to tell me we're split up, but you still get to choose where I live? Do I hear you correctly?"

Jeremy doesn't answer. He removes a wrapped gift out of his black Army coat pocket and hands it to her. Then, sits with his legs gapped and leans in on his elbows. He doesn't want to miss their reaction.

"What's this, a parting gift?" Rahab asks, loosely holding the present.

Puah chuckles. *That's my girl.*

"Open it! Please," he demands anxiously.

Rahab unwraps the neatly wrapped box. A broad malicious smile spreads across Jeremy's face. He licks his lips in anticipation.

Weird. Rahab opens the box. "Ahh!" she screams, dropping everything and jumping on the sofa.

Jeremy laughs hysterically. What looks like two small balls fall splat and clumsily roll across the hardwood floor, stopping at Mr. Jenkins' feet. Puah jumps into his lap.

In the noisy chaos, Silas runs out of the bedroom.

Jeremy stands up. "Oh, you're home tonight, good. Now I only have to say this once."

Rahab gets down from the sofa and studies the bloody clumps. "Are those eyeballs?"

"Yeah, do they look familiar?" Jeremy asks; now looking like *Jack Nicholson* in *The Shining*, for real. He grabs Rahab's waist and pulls her into his arms. She hesitates but is careful not to upset him or Silas. "They're the last thing I saw...wide and staring. Icy blue."

Sweat rolls down his temple, and he quickly wipes it away.

"Are they actually from someone's eye sockets?" Puah asks, examining them from Mr. Jenkins' lap.

"Nothing gets past you, huh? Yuh nuh memba dem?" Jeremy probes. "He remembered you and your mother."

"Jeri, is that T-John?" Rahab yells. She stares in shock at the man she once shared her life with, the man she held at night and felt safe enough to close her eyes, the man she thought she knew. *No, he wouldn't go this far, would he?*

"Now there's no hard feelings between us," Jeremy whispers, cupping her face gentler than he has possibly ever done.

He softly kisses her swollen lip, sucking it tenderly. Rahab rests her hands against his firm chest, first in defense, then in sorrow. They briefly stare into each other's eyes. Hers are full of tears. The fire is extinguished. His are conflicted and finally showing signs of life. His chest hurts.

In a while, he'll be making more money than he's ever dreamt of, and yet, it doesn't feel as good as he imagined. Rahab won't be there to share it with. He can hear Canaan's voice telling him that there will be other women. *But none like her, my partner.* Jeremy releases her both mentally and physically then turns toward the family, eyeing Silas in particular. He can sense he wants to hit him, and he can't blame him.

"I want all of yous out of my building by two o'clock tomorrow. I hired a moving company. They'll be here by noon." He surveys the room and enjoys seeing the shock on everyone's faces. "They'll be equipped with whatever you need, and you can take whatever you want from here."

"Are you serious?" Rahab asks, taking back her sorrow.

He doesn't answer. He's said all he has to say.

"It's been my extreme pleasure, peasants," Jeremy rudely adds, smiling figuring he can't depart on a pleasant note. He turns on his *beef and broccoli* colored *Timbs* to leave but stops short.

"Si, don't forget about that furniture delivery we talked about. They should be here tomorrow around the same time as the moving company. Unlock the back gate and direct them to the elevator. Key them in, they know the rest."

"Yup," Silas dryly answers, feeling uninclined to help him. He could care less about Jeremy or his furniture.

"Cool."

Jeremy strides out of the apartment allowing the door to slam behind him. The scent of his *CK One* lingers and, if you listen hard enough with your imagination, you can hear his anthem *"C.R.E.A.M"* by *Wu-Tang Clan* trailing behind him.

Chills run up Rahab's arms. Her heart tells her to *say goodbye.*

I AM RAHAB

THE WALL TUMBLES DOWN

JC MILLER

A MESSAGE

Rahab called Salmone as soon as Jeremy left. He was in the field, so she shared with his comrades what she felt was vital information about the moving and delivery trucks coming to the building. Jeremy had already paged Salmone and Kaleb asking that they free their schedules tomorrow around the same time. The dots were connecting, and a major deal was happening at Jeri Cole's.

"It's late you should make doe-doe," Salmone expresses over the phone to Rahab's laughter. His Louisiana Creole jargon both tickles and comforts her.

"I should go to bed, but I can't sleep." Her freedom is around the corner, and it's both exciting and frightening.

"This time tomorrow, life as you know it will be forever changed. How do you feel about that?" Salmone asks, concerned about Rahab's mental stability. She puts up a good front, but he knows she's a nervous wreck. *They all must be.*

"I don't know if it's all sunk in yet. Sometimes, I wanna scream and cry. Other times, I feel like laughing. I am happy though. I'm definitely happy this is going to be over."

"Cool, everything else will fall into place. It's gonna be a long process. You're gonna go through a lot of different emotions. That's normal. Be kind to yourself. Allow the emotions to happen."

"Thank you. I'm glad to hear that I'm finally somewhat normal," she jokes.

"Hey, I talked to my parents today."

"Oh my gosh, how are they doing? I've been so caught up I haven't even asked about anyone," Rahab chokes up at the thought of home and those left behind.

"They're great. When I told them we found each other, Pa started speaking in tongues..." A broad smile spreads across Rahab's face. "...and Maw-Maw and Ma mostly cried."

"Ooh, I miss them so much," she confesses, tearing up. "I don't know how I got in this mess. It feels like my life has been set on *jacked up* since Big Mama passed. I don't even know who I am anymore. I'm afraid, Sal."

"I know, Rah; it's a scary situation."

"It is, but I'm not scared about tomorrow. I feel confident that God's got this. *THIS* is way beyond me; I know that now. What I'm afraid of is starting over. What am I gonna do? How will I live? I've been thinking about pursuing dance again, but honestly, I don't know if I want it anymore. I think I lost the desire."

"That's understandable. You've been through a lot. And you know what? There's no rush. All that stuff will be waiting when you're ready." Salmone knows that *he and God* have other plans for her.

"Nah, not in this industry. You get old fast out here. You gotta stay on top of the game and keep yourself relevant. Hey, speaking of relevant; I was wondering, how is it that you never saw any of my videos or heard of Voodoo Doll before? We could have reunited a long time ago."

"Well, you don't exactly look like yourself," he truthfully blurts.

"Ouch!"

"But! I've heard of Voodoo Doll, I knew she was Cole's girl. I've seen pictures. I may have even seen a video.

I just didn't recognize you. I'm still that awkward PK you know. I'm not really into the hip-hop scene."

"What? Hip-hop is life."

"Nah, it's all about zydeco, boo." They laugh, Rahab harder than he.

"I'm kidding," he clarifies, not wishing for her to believe that he's that dry.

"I hope so, although I find it hard to imagine you getting ya *tootsie roll* on."

"What! Please, girl. Ah be killing dem *Tootsie Rolls*. Especially dem fruit-flavored joints. Green apple. Dat's my shiznic," Salmone jokes.

"Yeah, that sounds about right," she speculates, dabbing tears caused by laughter away.

"Nah, but seriously, now that we've reunited I'm positive I've seen a poster circulating in the locker room before." He doesn't want to invade Rahab's privacy or her comfort with him but wants to know.

"Yeah, you probably did," she confirms, wincing. She's not proud of the decision anymore. "I did a few risqué shots a few years back. Jeri wanted something to circulate but quickly changed his mind after its success. He said it made me too accessible. I was getting a little too popular for his comfort."

"Sounds like a jealous lover."

"I don't know what he is. In the beginning, it was all about luring customers to Vixens. Then, when the attention got *too real,* to the point where I was being offered multiple deals excluding him, he flipped and had me focus on training the girls. I don't know if that was jealousy or protecting his investment."

"Maybe a little of both," Salmone inputs, feeling *some way* himself knowing nude pictures of her exist.

"I guess. I gave up trying to figure him out. We're both a hot mess." She admits her faults but doesn't want to go down that road. She's already feeling guilty about being on the wrong end of the law. Rahab quickly changes the topic. "Do you ever wish you could go back in time?"

"Yeah, maybe a little more than I should." He wishes he could go back and erase some of her past.

"Remember the good ole days of fishing, skipping rocks, and me beating you at whatever we were doing?" They laugh, reminiscing.

"Ah don't know bout all dat winning stuff, but yeah. Cherishing those moments kept me looking for you. They kept me searching and praying when everyone else said to give up."

"I'm glad you didn't," Rahab responds, feeling her layers peel back. "Tell me about yourself," she asks, changing the topic yet again. "It seems you know everything about me. What have you been up to…any kids? Wifey at home?" *Yikes, what if he does?* She assumed he was still *just Sal*.

"Nope. None of dat."

Whew!

"I'm really just a focused guy. You already know what I do for a living. Ahh, let's see. I joined the *Army Reserve* after high school. I was in *Desert Storm*."

"Oh, my goodness, really?"

"Nothing life-threatening, but after that, I realized how short life truly is. So, I moved to New York determined to find you. I became a cop, and the rest is history," Salmone reveals, not wanting to sound creepy but she is his life.

"Through all of that, you mean to tell me you're not booed-up?"

"Nope."

"A nice-looking single guy with a solid career. What the heck is happening in the real world?" She finds Salmone's story impossible to believe.

The girls at the club would be all over him.

Salmone nervously laughs. "To be completely honest, no one compares to you. And I hate to sound corny or whatever, but you are my first and only true love." He exhales deeply. The statement took a significant load off.

"Wow! I'm speechless," She nervously giggles. She hasn't felt like a schoolgirl in years, and her innermost thoughts know that the feelings are reciprocated.

"Listen, our worlds may not blend with a typical love song, and most likely they don't even match the beauty the Lord has playing against them, but I—"

"I'm no saint!" Rahab abruptly interrupts, feeling an overwhelming conviction and need to come clean. She knows where he's going.

"Rah."

"Let me finish, Sal."

"I'm a sworn officer of the law, please remember that," he interrupts, warning her and regretting his honesty.

"I know, and the Prince of Judah. How can I forget?" She acknowledges what she perceives as perfection. "Whatever I say may be used against me, I know, but I'm not clean. I'm running around here acting like a secret agent, and honestly, I've done my dirt. I scout women for Jeri; innocent, unsuspecting women. I introduce them to him, and after he wins them over with his money and his charm, I train them. I show them how to be cunning, seductive, and venomous like snakes. Who am I to want

Jeri behind bars? I deserve the cell next to him. If he's a Kingpin, I'm the Queen."

"Were any of the women under age?"

"NO."

"Were they taken against their own free will or forced to take mind-altering substances?"

"No."

"No? Okay, then you're a pawn just like them. I deal with men like Cole all the time. They're the ones who are cunning. They make people believe what they want them to believe."

"Sal, we were partners."

"Oh yeah? Did you receive equal pay? Is there a paper trail in your name? Have you ever signed any legal or binding documents? Did he pay you for training, scouting, dancing, and whatever else you did?" Salmone interrogates, assuming his title and becoming harsh. He's been searching for her for years. He knows there's no paper trail.

"Jeri took care of me and my family. We never wanted for anything."

"Oh, I'm thinking *partnership* meaning a legal form of business between two or more individuals sharing management and profits. You mean *life partners*, but still, you do have access to bank accounts, debit cards, or joint accounts, right?" he asks, patronizing her.

"No," she whispers.

"You were a pawn, Rah. He pimped you hard just like he pimped all the others. I'm sorry."

Rahab falls silent as the past six years replay in her mind. She's heard everything that Salmone is saying before, but it never stung like this.

He's right. Jeri played me...because he knew all I wanted was security.

Salmone briefly removes the cell from his mouth, glad that he used his personal phone. He's roused himself and ushered feelings about Rahab that he's been trying to suppress. Rah, *why did you do this to your life? Lord, how do you push past the fact that the woman you love is a stripper?* He doesn't want to acknowledge her in that light. He wants to love who she was.

"I'm sorry, Rah," he states sincerely, bringing the phone back to his mouth.

"Sorry for what? You didn't do anything. I'm the fool. I'm the one caught up in this mess."

"Don't beat yourself up; Cole's manipulative."

"It's no wonder God wanted nothing to do with me." Rahab readies herself to enter a full-blown pity party. "He found pity on Le-Le and Si, maybe even Minton. They were helpless but not me. I prey on the helpless. How can God use me?"

"He has *saved us and called us with a holy calling not according to our works, but according to his own purpose and grace.* God has an ultimate plan for us all. Do you have a Bible?" Salmone asks, remembering the calling to save his friend before the claiming of a wife.

"Lydia and Silas do, but I don't wanna wake them," she answers, allowing defeat to creep in.

"**What about your Big Mama's treasure?**" A reminder comes upon her.

"I do have a Bible!" she proclaims, remembering the metal box she passes over in the wooden chest when making her Big Mama's oils. "Hold on, Sal."

Rahab quietly taps on Puah's bedroom door. Lotti's chest is in her closet. No one answers, so she gently pushes the door open. The running television reveals a snuggled couple. A smile widens Rahab's face as she slips into the room. If she were to turn the television off Puah would wake up, and it's good to see her at rest. Her relationship with Mr. Jenkins is *a* far cry from her days with Minton. *New relationship goals.* Rahab gets down on her knees to rummage the chest. She gently removes a metal box and tips out of the room.

"I got it, Big Mama's Bible," she excitedly yells toward the mobile phone laying on the sofa as she opens the box. A picture of Lotti, Richard, and Mags at T-Ray's greets her, and she loses herself in reverie.

"You okay?" Salmone asks, hearing soft sniffles.

His question is drowned-out. Rahab covers her mouth to stifle her wailing. She slowly re-reads an inscription handwritten and dated by Lotti days before her death once more for accuracy.

My dearest Rahab,

This is my greatest treasure and I believe every word. My only prayer is that God will love you more than I. This ole gal is stubborn and stuck in her foolish ways, but there's hope for you. I had a dream last night and I fear my days are short.

God said to me, I have worn myself out trying to clean the boiling pot. Even the fire can't take away its thick tarnish. I tried to clean you of your filthy lust, but you wouldn't clean yourself from your filth. You will never be clean until I unleash my fury on you. The LORD has spoken, and I regard it as truth.

Lord knows my ways will never change, but there's hope for you. Pass on the boiling pot. Its history has meant us nothing but harm. This here is all you'll ever need. His grace is enough.

Love Always, Big Mama

"Rah?" Sal yells now concerned. She's whimpering.

"I'm okay," Rahab finally responds, sniffling and double breathing like a baby after a long cry. She picks up the phone. "I'm okay," she repeats, flipping through the marked and folded pages in search of more notes. She is disappointed in herself for taking so long to discover the message but elated that her grandmother knew the truth. "Sal, Big Mama believed! She sounded a lot like me...troubled." Salmone remains silent he's not quite sure of Rahab's rambling, but he's glad she's okay. "I can't believe this message has been here all this time, and I missed it over and over again because it was in a Bible."

"Maybe you did, but God's always on time," Salmone relates, binding the conversation together.

"You're right because I really needed this now." She wipes tears away.

"Can you do me a favor before we continue?"

"Anything," Rahab responds, feeling she owes him.

"Can you please open all of the curtains and blinds. I can't see you."

"Sal, are you outside?" Rahab jumps up and whips back the heavy drapery then opens the blinds that Puah has adorning the living room windows that open into a sunken level, brick wall enclosed, maintenance courtyard. She prefers a dark house when watching her television, that, and the scenery of a brick courtyard wall isn't the prettiest.

"I'm not too far," Salmone discloses, smiling at the sight of her in the pink robe. "I can protect you better if I can see you, my love."

Excited, Rahab waves into the darkened night. Her heart flutters knowing he's there.

I AM RAHAB

Look at me, I'm falling so in love.

JC MILLER

TRUMPETS

When the trumpets sounded, the army shouted, and at the sound of the trumpet, when the men gave a loud shout, the wall collapsed; so everyone charged straight in, and they took the city.
Joshua 6:5

Jeremy quickly jerks sitting straight up in bed. His body is covered in sweat. The trumpet in his dream sounded so realistic. He frantically scans the dimmed bedroom. Nothing appears out of place except the woman lying beside him. He harshly shakes her shoulder as he tries to recall her identity.

"Whaa?" she whines, half asleep.

"Get out," he crudely orders, remembering her from the lobby when he came in from having Chinese. *A hoodrat.* He wipes the sweat from his brow. *Yo, I gotta get this checked out.* His bed sheets are soaked in perspiration.

"You aight?" the woman, now awake, asks as she turns over to cuddle.

"Didn't I say get out?"

"Yeah, but I thought that maybe..."

Jeremy blankly stares at her. She isn't even that cute. *What the heck was I thinking?*

She sucks her teeth as she rolls out of bed and gathers her belongings, purposely leaving her thong behind. "Bye," she snaps, giving her exit her best sashay.

He isn't impressed. Today the last merged shipment of cocaine is due to arrive, and he feels like he's mentally falling apart.

A trumpet sounds again.

I AM RAHAB

"What the...I thought I was dreaming."

Jeremy hops out of bed and clumsily runs to the window. What appears to be a religious organization is assembled across the street from his building and they are marching along the sidewalk.

"Yo!" he yells, opening the window. "It's too early for this crap. God ain't even up yet." He slams the window and notices the time. It's 5:46 in the morning. "Dang."

JC MILLER

RISE AND GO

Pastor Josh boarded a plane to New York City shortly after speaking to his son. He's confident that Salmone is professionally capable of handling his career, but his spirit told him to **rise and go**. Rahab is a touchy subject. Her absence altered Salmone's life. Her reappearance is guaranteed to change it forever. Pastor Josh isn't on a babysitting mission, rather a spiritual conquest.

Upon his arrival, he contacted a sister church and organized a prayer alliance. As fate would have it, the church belonged to Pastor Paul, and Silas had previously briefed him on the situation. They were already in prayer. Heading to the streets was the next step.

The community wanted their neighborhood and children back from the outpour of drugs flooding the area. Men like Jeremy controlled the corners. They stripped young girls of dignity and doped young men with pipe dreams. The plan was to march around the blocks surrounding Palm Court, Jeremy's building.

The group started small. Twelve people prayed quietly yet earnestly as they walked. By 5 am, one bullhorn and a trumpet later, more people joined. When they reached Palm Court again, the horn was blown as a confirmation to *stay woke*, the underlying message to the *city that never sleeps*.

"Claim back your childr'n. Claim back de streets. Heavenly Father, ah lift deez streets up to you. De thief only comes to steal, kill, and destroy. He's stolen our childr'n. He's taken dem from under us, Lord!" Pastor Josh affirmed in a thunderous voice over the early morning city happenings.

He alerted the natives, infuriating some while motivating others. The assembly laid hands on buildings and known crack houses. They stopped and prayed for prostitutes and druggies roaming the streets in search of life, then ushered them into the assembly, not caring to leave anyone behind. The group grew.

JC MILLER

A DOOR OF HOPE

"Morning, Rah. Did you sleep at all?" Puah asks, walking into the kitchen. The smell of *cafe con leche* and bacon woke her.

"I got a few hours. How about yourself?"

"I slept amazingly," Puah answers, noticing Lotti's Bible opened on the table. "Where did you find this? I haven't seen it in years."

"It was in the lock-box in the chest. Sal and I did some reading last night. Hey, did you know about the inscription inside?"

Puah takes a seat in front of the Bible. She's ashamed to say she hasn't touched it since she was a child flipping through it in search of hidden money.

"You and Sal seem to be picking up where you left off, huh?" She remarks before turning to the cover page then smiling at the sight of Lotti's perfect penmanship.

"Yeah, it seems that way," Rahab answers, blushing. Her feelings for Salmone are read upon her face although she isn't ready to admit them.

"Hmm, I didn't know about this," Puah responds, reading the timely message but appearing unaffected. "Wow, deep."

"Remember what that practitioner told us Big Mama said before she passed...something about *everything* I needed to survive?"

"Yeah, sort of," Puah answers, not wanting to go down that road so early in the morning. She's been respecting Rahab's fragile condition, *but enough is enough.*

"God is *the* "everything" Big Mama was talking about."

I AM RAHAB

"I find that hard to accept. Mama was no religious junky," Puah answers, doubtful that her mother believed in anything other than her potions.

"No, she wasn't, but she did believe," Rahab notes, determined in believing that her newly found faith has a foundation drenched in prayer.

"You know, Mama read this book every night before bed," Puah relates, feeling slightly sentimental. "And every night before bed she reminded me that I was beautiful in spite of all the white faces we lived amongst. She encouraged me to stay smart and never allow anyone to be my mind, but she never mentioned following a religious path. She did, however, concoct potions and gris-gris bags. All I'm saying is, when you believe in something, it usually shows up in your life."

Rahab nods, agreeing. "Maybe, she was kinda working things out, or maybe her faith didn't require any religious charades."

"Or maybe Mama romanticized over this book like a good novel. It does have your typical heroes, villains, and such." Puah closes the Bible. It has no home in her heart. Rahab wonders if they read the same inscription.

"I don't believe that's possible, Pu. These words are living. You can't read this book in its entirety and not be forever changed or question your existence. Big Mama believed, and that's everything to me right now," Rahab proclaims, remembering what Salmone taught her about being saved. *If you believe in your heart in the Lord Jesus, you shall be saved.* Now she imagines Lotti in a better place as opposed to a cold grave. "Besides, Big Mama would never tell me anything she didn't believe one hundred percent. Especially on her deathbed."

Puah expresses some agreeance but accepting the obvious would require a total change in mindset. Rahab moves the Bible and places a cup of coffee in front of her mother, followed by a breakfast sandwich. Saving Puah from their oppressed lifestyle isn't her only goal anymore. She now wants to save her eternally.

"That woman also mentioned that Big Mama said to *pass* on the boiling pot, and Big Mama states it here," Rahab adds, taking a seat and opening the old pew Bible to the inscription. Puah lifts an eyebrow as she bites into the sandwich. She puts her faith in Señora Martha's tarot cards more than anything else. "I believe what she's saying is to renounce Voodoo and instead believe in Jesus, who is greater."

"Mama believe in some blue-eyed devil? Nah, I'ma have to stop you right there," Puah blurts, only knowing the Jesus that adorned the dining room wall at the Fontaine's estate.

Rahab sucks her teeth. "Now you know I'm not talking about no Easter Bunny, Santa Claus, Hollywood Jesus. That's make-believe. I'm talking about Christ the Lord. The son of GOD, Almighty. The creator and ruler of the universe. Somebody greater! Someone who loves me in my *wretchedness* just as much as he loves an innocent baby."

"I don't know," Puah doubts, sipping on her hot coffee. "God ain't never been there for me. We're a million miles away from each other."

"Do you believe He's here now?" Rahab probes, feeling His presence lingering in the stillness of the room, in the humbling of her stature, and in the hairs rising on the back of her arms. Puah shrugs her shoulders and twists her mouth. Something is happening. She can't deny that. "God *will* deliver us from this mess, and He *will* give us a new life," Rahab faithfully proclaims.

"That's a lot to take in and you know I'm stubborn," Puah admits, popping a piece of bacon in her mouth. "But, these past few days have been full of surprises. Speaking of surprises..." she changes the subject ready to end the conversation; she's had enough. "...shouldn't we be getting things in order for the movers?"

"I don't have anything except Big Mama's chest," Rahab replies, taking the hint that her time on the topic is up.

"Girl, what about all that fancy stuff upstairs? You can have your God but don't be a fool," Puah advises, intending on taking everything she owns and some things she doesn't. Although she dislikes Jeremy, she's comfortable with his expensive gifts.

"I don't want it," Rahab reveals, intending on starting over. She opens the Bible and pretends to read. She can feel a full-blown argument brewing. Puah gives her the side-eye.

"Rah, you worked hard for that stuff."

"Well, it's all a part of a criminal investigation now. All *that stuff* was bought with blood money. It doesn't belong to me anymore."

Puah stares at her like she has two heads. *My baby's being brainwashed.* "You do know that there's life after this?" She sarcastically informs Rahab. "You gonna get a job wearing that pink robe? I know you have that twenty grand, but..." Rahab shakes her head no. "What do you mean, no?" Puah asks, rolling her neck.

"I'm turning in the money," Rahab whispers, now playing over her breakfast sandwich.

Puah chokes and starts coughing uncontrollably. "You what?" she asks, pushing Rahab's patting hand off of her back.

"The police already have it in evidence, and while we're on the subject, you should know that unless the deal doesn't happen today, we're not moving into Jeremy's fancy apartment downtown. Sal has arranged a temporary safe haven."

Puah gets up from the table. She can understand the safe haven, but the money has got her floored.

"And after the safe haven what happens?" She pushes her chair under the table. "I'm caring for a man who is wheelchair bound and a child with special needs. What are we supposed to do?" Puah places her dishes in the sink. "Oh yeah, I know, wait on the Lord."

"Pu, you're losing sight of what's important. This is about our safety. Yes, everything else will fall into place. I have some money saved up from selling the oils, and don't forget Big Mama's money—"

"That you can't touch until next year around this time!" Puah knows that she shouldn't care about money this much, but it does *make the world go round.*

"Good morning," Gomer happily sings, entering the kitchen. "Guess who's going home today?"

"At least you got a home to go to," Puah snaps, rolling her neck. She sucks her tongue and leaves the kitchen.

"Okaay? What was that about?" Gomer asks, pouring herself a cup of joe.

"Never mind her, what's this about going home?" Rahab questions. Gomer is wearing a glowing smile.

"I just got off the phone with Zee," she sings, speaking of her husband, Hosea. "Don't worry; I didn't mention anything about the cops or the deal."

Salmone advised not to communicate pertinent information to anyone. He also cautioned about using the landline and Rahab's cell because of Jeremy's access to them.

"I spilled my guts, Rah-Rah," Gomer confesses, popping bread into the toaster. Everyone is aware of Gomer's street life, but she denies the truth out of pride. "I came clean about the drugs, the prostitution, the lies, everything, even about Jeri," she adds, looking back at her sister shame-faced.

Rahab's mouth falls open in disbelief. Gomer's never said these things out loud before. *She seems sincere. That is if she's telling the truth.*

Gomer has a habit of lying through her teeth while *honey drips off her lips.*

"I finally told him how I really feel about him, but I think Zee knows my heart better than I do at this point," Gomer airs, pulling out a chair to join her sister. "I don't know what happened but yesterday when you were sharing your story something clicked. I've felt conviction before, Lord knows I get preached to enough, but this was different." She takes Rahab's hand. "It was me seeing myself through your pain. You weren't preaching at me; you probably didn't even know you were sermonizing my soul. I'm not all bad."

"Sweetie, I know you're not." Rahab cups her little sister's hand, squeezing it tightly. "I know who you are; we did share a bed together for years." They chuckle, but the statement is true. Rahab has seen Gomer fight herself through nightmares.

"When I'm acting out...that's me punishing myself for being...me. Unworthy. Unworthy of Zee. Unworthy of the kids. Spoiled and manipulative Princess Go-Go. Yesterday, you helped me to see that what I'm doing isn't running, or self-medicating, or payback. It's hurtful, and it's time that I start facing my demons. I also learned that in spite of myself, this God that Zee is always talking about still loves me, and He'll see me through. I don't have to live this wounded life anymore. I don't want to. I can freely love Zee and not feel unworthy." Gomer's voice cracks as she tries to hold back tears. "I love him." Tears blink from her eyes. "I've hurt him so badly and I'm sorry. I wanna go home and hold my husband and kids and start over."

"What did Zee say?" Rahab anxiously asks.

"He cried. I cried. Then, he told me to come home. He said I'm his forever. I don't understand why this man love me so?" Gomer sings, standing to get her toast.

"He's an example of God's love, I guess," Rahab relates from her spirit. Gomer kisses her forehead.

"Thank you...and I'm so sorry I—"

"Don't, it's over. I love you."

"I love you too." Gomer sits down and embraces her sister's hand again. "That's why I want to *officially* apologize. You're everything to me, my beautiful big sister. I've been jealous, unruly, harsh...*big meany*." They laugh. "But seriously, from day one you've never changed. Your love has been consistent, and I've been a consistent brat. You don't deserve what I've said or done to you over the years. I'm sorry."

"Thanks, Go. That means the world to me." Gomer pats Rahab's hand and smiles. "So, you mentioned you're leaving today?"

I AM RAHAB

"Well, I'm not about to leave you guys in this mess. I'm staying until we're all safe. Is the plan the same as last night?"

"Yeah," Rahab answers, standing to refresh her cup. She's tired but can't sleep. "We'll let the movers in and delay them as long as possible, let them pack *ALL* this stuff. Hopefully, before the actual move, we'll know something. Sal is dead-set against us moving to another Jeri location. He got us a safe haven and a storage company. Whatever we need he says."

"Cool. You like this Sal guy, huh?" Gomer questions, nudging Rahab's arm.

"He's a really good friend," Rahab answers, blushing again.

"Mhmm, I know about those *really good friends*. I remember the stuff I use to do to Zee when we were kids." They laugh in remembrance.

"No, you were just nasty. Sal and I were innocent kids. I may wanna do a few of those things now though," Rahab admits, feeling embarrassed. She's trying to put aside her *wayward ways*.

"I knew it! It's in the DNA," Gomer hollers, laughing. "You want him, don't you?"

Rahab covers her red face. "I do, and I feel horrible about it."

"Why? If it's who I think it is, he's fine as all get out," Gomer states, tickled by her big sister's bashfulness.

Rahab sighs, uncovering her face. "I feel like a floozie. I mean, in spite of all that's happening, I just feel stupid, like I should be a little more focused on our next step. Like Pu said, where are we going to live? What are we going to do? Sal makes me feel...warm and fuzzy inside."

"Mhmm!" They laugh.

"Not like that...entirely. I mean safe. Loved."

"He sounds like my Zee." Rahab nods, agreeing.

"Rah, I'm no life coach, but it seems to me you're entitled to this. You've spent too many years trying to love Jeri and trying to make him love you in return. Then there's us hooligans. Look at the years you've invested. That mental vacation is whassup! In the words of my Hosea, *'God is the only one who can make the valley of trouble a door of hope.'*"

Rahab tilts her head in amazement. "When did you get so smart?"

"A few minutes ago." They laugh again. "Seriously, there's nothing like being with someone who loves you completely, and I can't remember you ever having that, Rah. You're twenty-four. Live a little."

"You're right," Rahab agrees, pondering over her life. "Hey, I've been debating over something, but I think I'm ready now. Can you help me?"

Rahab was hurt when Salmone said *she didn't look herself.* She thought of him searching for her all those years, and Voodoo Doll being right there in the public eye and he didn't recognize her as his friend. The more she thinks about it, the more she understands. She hardly knows who she is anymore.

"Anything, sis," Gomer responds. "What is it?"

"You feel like playing with my hair like you used to? I wanna cut it and let my natural hair color grow out."

I AM RAHAB

VIRTUOUS WIFE

Silas and Lydia stand at the courtyard entrance gate waiting for Jeremy's delivery and the moving truck to arrive. Feeling both anxious and cold, Silas holds Lydia tightly wrapped inside of his *Carhartt* jacket. *She's a trooper*, he thinks of his virtuous wife, pulling her wool beanie down over her ears and kissing her forehead. It's a bitterly cold day.

Lydia begged to help with the delivery, and initially, Silas rejected her wishes, having no clue of the possible danger.

"You heard what Rah said," he told her. "Stay in the house. If anything goes wrong, I would never forgive myself."

"Papi, if you go down I go down. Period," Lydia insists. She didn't want him out there alone. Jeremy was jealous hearted and still had it out for Silas. *It could be a set-up.* "Seer-vee-ously, Si, I'd die without you," she declared in her thick Bronx Latina accent. "Let me go with you. I need to be by your side. Nothing is going to happen." Lydia pleads, teary-eyed. She held a secret within herself and wanted to make sure he was around.

"Stop talking crazy, Bugs. Krystal needs her mother," Silas demands, not wanting to hear crazy talk.

"God, forgive me, but there is no me without you. Baby girl would be motherless either way."

"You're a hard-headed woman."

"And you love me," Lydia asserts, wrapping her arms around his waist and resting her head against his chest. He cradles her small body in his strong arms and rocks her gently. "After both trucks arrive, we'll go in the house and stay put until we hear from the cops. Nothing is going to happen to either of us, but neither of us is leaving each other's side today," she adds, intently staring in his face.

Silas puckers his lips and leans in as she tiptoed to kiss him. His heart belongs to her.

"You do know that I'm supposed to be the head over our house, right?"

"You are...and my heart desires to house you."

"I'm gonna house your heart alright," Silas jokes, tickling her waist.

Lord, you've brought us this far. He inwardly prays, sighing deeply. *Please protect us. Not a hair harmed on my family's heads.*

Against the families' dilemmas and lifestyle changes, Silas and Lydia have remained. It's not duty that keeps them tightly wound, it's love. Silas, a *faithful brother*, devotes himself to his family's protection. Certain dynamics hold the Auguste/Williams family together. Lydia understands them. Where would she be without the loyalty of those said dynamics? As an entrepreneur, *not slothful in business, fervent in spirit, and serving the Lord*, Lydia now makes more than enough to afford a home. Money isn't the problem anymore. They would never abandon one another. It's been her and Silas' prayer that Rahab finds her worth in Christ Jesus, along with the strength to leave Jeremy.

I AM RAHAB

GHETTO HEAVEN

Jeremy stands by a window in deep thought. He's awaiting the drug lords to begin filing into his building. *This day can't end soon enough.* He notices the demonstrators starting another lap around the neighborhood. They've circled the area at least six times in the past six hours and, as much as they are annoying, he kind of hopes they stick around until after the exchange over. They add a certain orchestrated chaos.

"You're falling apart, kiddo," Canaan announces from his seat at the head of a conference table.

The casino deal is the deal of Canaan's lifetime. He's dreamt of owning one since he was a kid in Brooklyn pretending to be *Bugsy Siegel*. All of his mob stained affairs hail from his idol. Casino ownership is the final endeavor. He's never successfully managed to assemble the right people, enough finances, obtain the right property, and meet the tedious gambling control guidelines all at once. Finally, his ducks are in a row.

Canaan takes a long puff from his cigar. "This is the land flowing of milk and honey, baby. It don't get any better than this. What the heck is wrong with you?" He yells at Jeremy, who seems depressed. Canaan can't imagine stressing over a girl opposed to living out your dreams. "Pull yourself together, J-boy."

Jeremy managed to control the sweating issue. He took a cold shower and had a big breakfast at *Jimmy's Luncheonette* on Clay Avenue. He stopped by *Pelham Parkway Assisted Living* to give an old acquaintance an early Christmas gift and play a few hands of Gin Rummy. Then, he got himself a *fresh James cut* and honed his debating skills while engaging in barbershop politics. He rounded off his morning indulging in a little nose candy. He thought he was alright, but apparently, he was wrong.

"You still got that harlot on your mind?"

"Pfft, please! I'm over that," Jeremy answers his mentor, popping his collar and rolling his shoulders. "I'm moving onto bigger and better things," he continues, spotting the first set of connections entering the building.

Canaan knows he's lying. He practically raised him. "I know you, Jeri. You get caught up on them tit-feeding maternal types, it's no good for the business," Canaan states, waving his cigar as he talks with his hands.

"Pfft! You don't know what you're talking about, old-head," Jeremy insists, taking a seat and elevating his feet on the table.

"When you were a poor schmuck kid, do you remember how long it took me to stop you from crying over ya mommy?"

"How long, Pops?" Jeremy mockingly responds, entertaining the older Jewish man.

"Damn near three weeks. I almost gave up on you. I thought you'd never break," Canaan states, leaning into the table and staring at Jeremy.

Jeremy's mother, Yvonne, was an immigrant maid. She cleaned Canaan's Manhattan apartment every Saturday for fifteen years, amongst other things.

When her son got into a little mix-up, she knew of no one with money and connections but Canaan. Out on a desperate limb, she asked for his help. Canaan, feeling no obligation nor sympathy, obliged because he was looking for a kid for some running he planned in Brooklyn. He needed a smart kid, one he could teach and control from the inside. Yvonne often bragged about her son's accomplishments. Jeremy was her world. They lived alone on Nostrand Avenue in a one-bedroom flat. She slept on the couch giving her child the bedroom and everything else she never had growing up. Everything wasn't enough. Jeremy had a hankering for the finer things in life.

He studied the local drug dealers and aspired to surpass their success. He could have sought greatness like *John H. Johnson* or *Reginald F. Lewis,* but from his standpoint, ghetto heaven was easily obtained. He'd rather the fresh pair of *Puma Clyde's* sooner than later.

Jeremy's goal wasn't to be the two-cent hustler. He watched blaxploitation movies and read gangster literature by *Donald Goines* and *Iceberg Slim,* and idolized mobsters like *Frank Lucas.* Feeling confident in his study of the game, he set up his own business. Canaan found that impressive and reminiscent of himself.

Yvonne was supposedly killed by a hit and run driver leaving work one day, and Canaan conveniently took in the newly orphaned troubled teen. He made sure Jeremy finished his schooling at *Brooklyn Tech* and went on to graduate from Fordham *University's* business program.

Jeremy was no average hoodlum. He became Canaan's special project; the brain of the operation. The only problem was, he suffered from separation anxiety disorder. As a young boy, Jeremy claimed every tender-hearted girl as *the one,* but his lifestyle nor Canaan allotted him that pleasure. Manipulated breakups were like losing his mother over and over again until he finally accepted his mentor's advice and learned to love 'em and leave 'em.

Lately, Jeremy's been showing signs of distress again. To Canaan, it's an indication of the return of his anxieties. Rahab was a bad idea.

"That's what you're doing, you're crying over mommy."

"Chill! Don't guh dere, mon," Jeremy yells, sitting straight and removing his feet from the table. "Mom's got nothing to do with this."

"Yeah? Then why are you trying to screw this up by grieving over some chick? Everything we've ever done boils down to this. Do I eat alone? Have I ever held anything from you?"

"Nah! Stop bugging; I'm aight. I just have this haunting feeling I can't escape."

"Shake it off! This ain't an *Amityville Horror*! C'mon, J-baby. Everything I got I give to you," Canaan continues, rousing himself. "This is how you do me? Screw me over some female."

Jeremy wipes his brow. He's beginning to sweat again. "Our day is not screwed." He stands and straightens his black tracksuit jacket. "I ain't no sap-sucker either. This deal is going down."

"You darn skippy it's going down," Canaan agrees, invading Jeremy's personal space with his short stubby body. "And if it doesn't run as smoothly as a baby's bottom, something might happen to ya whore. Something to *really* grieve over just like with your mother."

"What the hell does that mean?" Jeremy replays the statement in his mind. *Was that a threat or a confession?* But before he can explore the comment further, the doorbell rings.

"Get the door," Canaan orders, turning to take his seat at the head of the table.

"What the heck did you mean by that, Mark?" Jeremy asks again, grabbing him by the arm. "You killed my mutha?" The thought enrages him.

"Don't be stupid." Canaan calmly answers. "Your mother was a terrific woman." Pulling his arm away and straightening his jacket before sitting, he continues, "I told you, she was the only Black I ever—"

"Don't!" Jeremy interrupts. He knows the gross details. Now, in his heart, he feels he knows the full story. He isn't a son of Mark Canaan, he's a part of his plan just like the other associates meeting today. Jeremy's head is swirling. He wipes his face with his sleeve.

"I'm lying; she wasn't the only one. There was that wall-slider on *Bleecker* in the seventies..." Canaan's walk down memory lane is interrupted by the doorbell ringing and pounding on the door. "Get the door, Jeri," he insists, getting aggravated. He's not sure Jeremy will make it, and that's unfortunate. "You better not screw this up."

"I said I'm good." Jeremy walks toward the door. *I'm alone in this world. It's time for the big payback.*

JC MILLER

THE DELIVERY

"Look, babe! I see a truck coming," Lydia announces, two minutes before schedule. It is a furniture company delivery truck.

As the drug lords eagerly wait to receive, cut, and distribute their portion of cocaine, the *Colombian* connection dressed as delivery men enter the rear of the building, *Fist of Fury* style.

Silas quickly opens the courtyard gate, pushing Lydia behind him. She shows no opposition but she's tuned-in to everything. The box-truck enters backward, following Silas' direction.

"You, Si-lass Willy-ams?" the grunge faced Hispanic man queries, holding a clipboard of paperwork.

"Yeah, that's me," Silas answers, noticing the man's partner is more interested in Lydia than the delivery. "You lost sumpin, part-nah?" Silas asks, annoyed at himself for allowing her to tag along. The guy smirks and returns to the truck to lower the ramp.

Silas gives *Clipboard Guy* the once over, broadening his shoulders then adjusting his skull-cap. He swipes his nose and twists his mouth while cupping his manhood. "Follow me," Silas firmly states after the male territorial dance is complete. He places Lydia in front of him and walks behind her. *Her dang coat is too short.*

Lydia can feel all eyes on her behind and is aware that her derriere has a walk of its own. She attempts to stiffen her gluteus muscles.

Don't make no sense. Silas continues to gripe inwardly, pressing the maintenance elevator button.

I AM RAHAB

The two helpers with *Clipboard Guy* approach them pushing a full-size sofa that is securely wrapped on a dolly.

"Jú think we can get ah'notter piece in dis elevator?" Clipboard asks.

"Yeah, man. Bring it," Silas answers, stalling the service elevator and keying-in Jeremy's floor.

"Yo, eses," Clipboard yells at his helpers who are staring and whispering about Lydia. "Put this in the elevator and go get the other piece," he orders in their native language. "Hurry. Ándale!"

The men laugh, pushing the sofa into the elevator. "I got something I want to put in her," one guy claims in Spanish as the other agrees.

Lydia crumples her nose in disgust and hides behind Silas. *Maybe I should've stayed in the house.*

"Tengo un tamaño trece de arranque para ese culo Mexicano apretado!" Silas responds to their surprise. What he said involves his size thirteen boot and an exit hole. Clipboard heartily laughs, slapping hands with Silas.

"Talk to ya boys, ese. Dat's my wife; I don't play that."

Clipboard nods in agreement. "Yo, stop playing around. Go get the other piece and leave this man's wife alone," he demands, winking at Lydia.

JC MILLER

SEVENTH ROUND

"Good afternoon, gentlemen. Who would like to be a millionaire today?" Clipboard announces, smiling brightly as he ushers his helpers in with the furniture. He sits his clipboard on the table and shakes hands with Canaan.

"Finally, my friend; you have made it to de big times," he states, quietly congratulating Canaan, patting him on the back. They go way back.

Solo and *Ky* quietly made the shipment handover and money exchange in a warehouse that morning. The drug deal, a *Transatlantic* affair, involves connections with Columbia and Italy. Clipboard and his crew took over the imported goods from the warehouse and slowly made their way to Palm Court, aka the stash-house, where all the drug lords were waiting on their cuts. Salmone and Kaleb followed behind the delivery truck making sure that there were no snags or delays.

"So, gentlemen, are we ready to get to business?" Canaan asks, returning to his seat at the head of the table.

"Heck yeah, that's what we here for," an associate yells.

"Then, let's get this party started." Canaan motions for Jeremy who then walks over to the two handcrafted Italian sofas, gesturing for Salmone and Kaleb to follow him. "Open it," he demands of the delivery men.

"¡Abrelo!" Clipboard translates.

The workers begin to unwrap the piece of furniture as per their bosses ushering. They're in a hurry to get to the next exchange. Everyone seems to lean-in as they carefully cut through the bubble wrap and then the fabric.

They slowly peel back the padding revealing ninety-four kilos of uncut cocaine-hydrochloride tucked in every corner of the sofa. Short gasps fill the space, quickly followed by crooked smiles and the rubbing of hands.

"Ahh, yeah! That's what I'm talking about, baby!" someone shouts, commencing declarations of excitement and agreement.

Before the workers begin to unwrap the next sofa, Jeremy gestures for Kaleb to examine and count the goods. The Columbians that Clipboard works with are reputable dealers, but for the associates' sake, they do a quick purity test. Kaleb removes a few random blocks and passes them to Salmone.

"Dis is de best. I guar-on-tee nine-tee seven percent purity," Clipboard broadcasts, lighting a cigar.

Salmone slowly runs a razor over a block and pulls back its covering, revealing solid rock cocaine. Smiling, he nods and declares, "This is legit." He then passes the block to an associate waiting to weigh out a piece for testing.

Suddenly, the trumpet sounds for the seventh and final time, and pagers begin to go off.

***

In front of Palm Court, Pastor Josh commands the assembly. "Shout! For the LORD has given you the city." The trumpet sounds and the assembly loudly begins to shout.

 They shout in rejoice.
 They shout in praise.
 They shout claiming victory.
 The shouting is heard by the entire community.

A SWAT team unexpectedly appears surrounding the entire area like a swarm of bees heading toward Jeremy's building. At first, the demonstrators are startled under the invasion but then realize that their prayers have been answered. A raid is taking place. They shout louder, drowning out the sound of sirens as the entry team barricades them away from the building. The neighborhood roars in chaos.

***

"Yo, 5-0 is in the area!" A few of the associates announce the presence of the police after checking their pagers. They have *falcons* looking out.

Everyone jumps up and quickly prepares to vacate the premises.

"You gotta be kidding me," Jeremy voices to no one in particular. His plans were foolproof, he's in shock.

"Exit rationally," Canaan instructs his associates over the commotion. "Use the stairs; both elevators are locked."

He then turns and yells at Jeremy, slightly startling him. "J-boy! Get the rest of that blow and drop it down the garbage shoot, then go fire up the furnace. Solo, Ky, help him!" He attempts damage control while whipping out his cell to make a call.

Jeremy begins to initiate orders but notices Canaan readying to leave with Clipboard. I'm not going down with my hands in the cookie jar while this old-school kosher-boy gets away. Nah!

"Mark!" He calmly walks over before Canaan exits the apartment. Thoughts of Canaan robbing him of a mother and a decent chance at life run through his mind. Jeremy impetuously pulls a gun on him.

"Do you know what you're doing?" Canaan asks, looking at the gun poked in his ribs. *Is this why he's been acting strangely.* He wonders if Jeremy is an informer.

"You and I are leaving together," Jeremy proclaims, nudging Canaan toward the door.

Suddenly, one of Clipboard's men takes a shot at them, missing them only by an inch. The history between Canaan and Clipboard goes too far back for either of them to leave separately. They're better dead than alive to *rat* on the operation. Jeremy grabs Canaan around the neck and uses his body as a shield. He shoots back and manages to kill one of Clipboard's men while Salmone shoots and disables the other. Jeremy and Canaan are worth more alive to the *NYPD*.

"I'm out! Y'all can stay here if you want," Jeremy yells. He heads for the stalled elevators. Salmone, Kaleb, and Clipboard follow. Halfway, Jeremy abruptly stops and turns, firing at them. He doesn't want their company. He unlocks the elevator and pushes Canaan inside, shooting once more before jumping in himself. "See ya, suckah!" he shouts as the doors close.

Salmone and Kaleb retreat to the staircase leaving Clipboard behind. The cell phone call that Canaan made earlier was for his helicopter. Clipboard heads to the roof.

"J-boy, what are you doing?" Canaan asks, trying to distract Jeremy's attention so that he can reach the hidden gun strapped to his leg. "We can walk out of here together if you follow my lead."

"Shut up!" Jeremy shouts, sending the elevator straight to the basement. "Always have an escape plan, remember that?" he mocks, referring to his detailed training. They'd both rather die than go to jail.

Jeremy has men monitoring Rahab's family's apartment. They were stationed there to make sure she stayed put. The movers are also his henchmen; there's a crate in the moving truck made especially for unexpected getaways. Jeremy pulls out his cell.

"Yo, 5-0 is in the area."

"Five-0 is in the building," the mover clarifies, not fully knowing the details but aware that they should always be on their toes. He saw the cops nosing around the courtyard from a bedroom window and locked the front door and ordered everyone to be quiet.

"Where y'all at?" Jeremy asks.

"O'Neil and Strong got detained at the truck while moving some boxes."

Frustrated, Jeremy shouts and punches the elevator wall. He was hoping he could slip into the truck without being noticed.

"What's the status of the apartment?" he then asks after a period of silence. He's pissed and can't see his way out of the dilemma unless he takes Canaan's offer. *But he can't be trusted.* Rahab comes to mind, as it seems she's never left it. *Maybe I can hide out in the apartment until things blow over.* He recalls the closet in the master bedroom has space hidden behind the wall.

"It's just me here," the henchman answers. "The men you posted at the door bolted when they heard the sirens. I got ya girl and her family in the house. We on the low. Yo, I ain't trying to go to jail, son. You need to get down here."

"I'm in the elevator," Jeremy dryly answers, ending the call. He wipes his forehead with the gunned hand. *I can't believe this is happening.* He feels he should have taken heed to what his body has been telling him. "Don't even think about it," he warns Canaan who's trying to reach for his hidden gun.

The elevator stops and, as the doors open, Jeremy swiftly grabs Canaan around the neck. "Now it's your turn to play along," he whispers, leading him out first and eyeballing the area. "Maybe if you're good you'll get out of here alive."

"It's not worth it, Jeri. It makes better sense to cop a plea. Dead bodies make a lawyer's job harder. Surrender," Canaan advises, whispering back.

"Shut up, old school. I ain't going to nobody's jail."

There's an eerie stillness in the air. The only noise is that of a rocking dryer hitting the cement floor in the laundry room and the muffled sound of sirens and shouting entering in from the closed courtyard door. Jeremy briefly closes his eyes and exhales deeply. *You are not going to jail,* he tells himself, sliding against a wall leading to the apartments.

"Freeze!" A cop yells as others simultaneously step out from behind every corner.

"I have a hostage," Jeremy conveys, continuing to slide against the wall.

"Please don't shoot," Canaan cries, his toupee flapping loosely over his eyes.

"You're surrounded, Cole. You may as well surrender," the cop suggests.

Jeremy heartily laughs as though having a mental breakdown. Perspiration builds upon his forehead. *At least they know my name.* He bangs on the door from which a scrap of scarlet sheet hangs with the back of his foot.

When it opens, he steps backward through it. At the sight of him, the women scream.

"I have hostages. You surrender," Jeremy mocks the cop, pushing Canaan back out into the hall. He's dead weight and no longer a father to him. Without warning, he shoots him in the back of the head and moves away from the closing door. Canaan never saw it coming. *That's all I owe you.*

For years, Jeremy orchestrated the more delicate details, and calculations of their mob influenced affairs, as well as running successful businesses. There's no doubt had he chosen another path life would have panned out differently. Had he known he'd end up in his current predicament, maybe he would have made better choices after graduating at the top of his class. Perhaps he would have taken the large offers from legitimate businesses that were thrown his way? His head was arrogant. His heart was darkened. He sought a world he could control. Would've, could've, should've.

HOSANNA! HOSANNA!

When Salmone and Kaleb finally reach the front lobby, they are arrested and detained along with the other drug lords. NYPD has all of them spread eagle on the floor, reading them their rights and searching them for evidence. Salmone hardly had time to notice his father shouting unto the Lord on his behalf, but his father saw him and cried out the more as the cops usher him and Kaleb into a squad car, handcuffed.

"I thought the plan was to rescue Rahab and her family before doing anything," Salmone angrily questions, noticing his colleague's guilty faces as he and Kaleb approaches.

The raid was premature. The squad car driver told Salmone and Kaleb that a helicopter was noticed circling the area. The team presumed it to be a lookout or getaway chopper. Not wanting to blow the opportunity to arrest everyone, they made the split decision to move in. Salmone and Kaleb, as the undercover cops, never received the opportunity to vacate the premises before executing the raid as customary.

"Suspect has accomplices working the inside of the apartment," an officer answers Salmone. "A hostage situation was inevitable."

"What's the status now?" Kaleb asks, to reign his partner in and keep him from dwelling on the change in plans.

"Cole and Ramirez are the only suspects not apprehended. Cole... is in the apartment," the officer regretfully states. "He now has six hostages and one dead body."

"What?" Salmone freezes. His heart drops.

He and Kaleb thought they heard a gunshot over the ruckus when they were being detained in front of the building.

"Do we know who?" Kaleb asks.

"Canaan," the cop reports. The officers all sigh.

They've been on this mission for over a year. No deaths are acceptable, but Canaan's is painful. He's their Jewish mob link.

"Are the riflemen in position?" Salmone questions, ready to assist before anyone else dies. "Jeremy's homicidal, we gotta hook him quick."

"There are three snipers," another cop responds, pointing out the locations.

"Okay good. All of the curtains and blinds should be drawn. The hostages are probably in the living room; it's the nearest area to the point of entry. Can we move a sniper behind that wall up there or inside of that truck?" Salmone gives out directions. The team doesn't question his leadership; they share the information. Time is of the essence.

Salmone grabs a pair of binoculars and walks off. The trucks parked in the courtyard are blocking the view of the apartment.

"Please, Lord," he whispers, pushing his disheveled hair from his face.

Kaleb lays a hand on his partner's shoulder. "Victory is ours today. Do you hear the chanting?"

Salmone forces himself to stop and listen. They all heard the trumpet and the shouts coming from upstairs. Jeremy excused it as *a very loud religious demonstration,* and it sort of became background noise.

"Hosanna! Hosanna!" the crowd yells. Salmone humbly lowers his head as his eyes moisten.

"Lord, we thank you and receive your protection over every person in this building today. Father, we faithfully trust in your name and give you all the honor and glory. Amen," Kaleb briefly prays, identifying the Lord's hand in the perceived chaos. Rahab is indeed his partner's wife, and the Lord is erasing all of her past.

"Amen," Salmone confirms, needing that reminder. His feelings have sidetracked him.

The love he has for Rahab has flourished in the last two days. The girl he adored has become the woman he can't live without. His arms itch to hold her. His body yearns to know her. His spirit desires to become one. Time no longer stands between them. Their future is a *drug bust* away.

Salmone presses his head against the cold bars of the courtyard gate. *There's nothing I can do right now but wait.* He tries to push the thought of Jeremy's *hair-trigger temper* out of his mind.

"De *insistent prayer of a righteous person is powerfully effective!*" Pastor Josh yells over the bullhorn before it's confiscated by a cop. His son must keep the faith. They all must. Salmone alertly perks up.

"Pa?"

JC MILLER

THE SMELL OF DEATH

"Jeri, what's happening?" Rahab queries, finding the courage to come out from amongst her huddled family.

Jeremy is pacing the floor and sweating like a pig. She's never seen him this anxious before. She attempts to rest her hand on his arm, but he quickly grabs and twists it before noticing her. She whimpers as he stares straight through her as though she's there, and not there at the same time.

"Go and sit with ya family," he coldly instructs before releasing her wrist and pacing again.

He's on his toes and thoughts usually flow easier when he's moving, but there's too much noise inside his head. Trying to come up with a plan seems useless, so he gripes over who set him up.

"I know Solo is a cop. I can feel it. But he helped me," Jeremy rambles. His strategy was seamless. *How did 5-0 find out? He has to be undercover.*

"What are we gonna do, Jeri? Ain't no way we walking outta here. We might as well give up before it gets worse," the henchman states nervously. It is the same request he's made five times in the past ten minutes. His pestering is annoying Jeremy. It's already hard enough for him to think.

"Give up? Shut up, I'm the one giving out orders here," Jeremy declares, pointing the gun at the flunky. "We jump when I say jump."

"Yo, watch where you point that, homie. Somebody might get hurt," the henchman warns, mindful not to aim back at his superior.

"What? Hurt like this?" Jeremy fires a shot.

I AM RAHAB

The henchman instantly jolts backward. The close-range bullet explodes and exits his chest, entering the wall behind him.

The room falls silent.

"Ain't no way *you're* walking outta here today, homie," Jeremy states, staring down at his longtime friend. They ran the streets in Brooklyn when they were kids. He momentarily starts to second-guess himself but then figures he's severing connections. "Anybody else want some?" he asks, turning toward the family.

The women instinctively lean in to cover Silas. They know he's a target. Jeremy begins to laugh. *All of these years of wanting to be the alpha male and I still can't supersede a crackhead.* He points his gun at each family member, mimicking a gunshot.

"One by one, I'ma knock you out," he threatens in a calm yet hostile tone. "Until you..." he aims at Rahab. "...have no other choice but to lean on me."

"Cole!" someone with a bullhorn shouts from outside of the front door. "We're prepared to negotiate."

Jeremy broadly smiles as though his situation has just changed. He walks toward the door keeping his eyes on the nervous family. He's out of range from the window.

"It's about time!" Jeremy shouts back.

"Is everyone okay, we heard a gunshot?" the negotiator asks.

"If you call dead okay, I guess we're good," Jeremy laughs, looking at the henchman's body laid against the wall, assessing he did him a favor.

"Listen, I'm Officer Smith. I'm going to try my best to accommodate you. Our goal is a peaceful conclusion. Please, we don't want any more killings. All that matters is safety and those innocent people," he states, distracting

Jeremy while a sniper enters the truck in front of the living room window which faces the courtyard. He lays across the seats aiming his gun through the cracked door.

Jeremy glances over at the family. "Innocent. Ha! You don't know these folks like I do."

They're the closest he's come to having a real family since his mother and sister passed. For a second, his heart increases in size as he considers what he's doing. Then, he realizes the cops have him where they want him, doubting himself. He proceeds to make his requests.

Observing the split-second change in Jeremy's demeanor, Rahab takes advantage and, against her family's pleading, she slowly gets up from the couch again. Jeremy gestures with his gun for her to sit down. He's working on negotiations with *the man.*

"Please, Jeri. Whatever it is, it's nothing that can't be worked out," Rahab softly reassures, continuing to walk toward him with her arms open in a welcoming manner. She's on eggshells, but she caught a glimpse of his heart. He allows her to move closer.

Something is different. Jeremy lowers his gun as she approaches. Her aura isn't sensual; it's peaceful. He'd been so distracted he hadn't noticed until now that she cut her hair. *The Halle Berry cut suits her.* His heart flops as he tenderly palms her bruised face. Rahab encloses his hand between her cheek and shoulder and his eyes begin to swell with tears. Her heart breaks. She's never seen him cry.

"What's happening with you?" she asks, taking his hand in hers. He instantly chokes up.

Stop, he admonishes himself like he used to as a child. *Tears are wasteful.* His plans are, do or die. His own life is a gamble. This feeling he's having has no place.

"So, do you want a helicopter or not?" Smith interrupts, waiting on Jeremy to finish his list of requests.

Jeremy successfully redirects his attention. "Yeah. I want a chopper to LaGuardia for me...and my girl," he spontaneously decides. "Then a private jet. Destination...will be disclosed later. And a million dollars in small unmarked bills." He intently stares into Rahab's eyes. His intellectual mind tells him, *you're playing the game of negotiations. This is as far as it gets.* He wishes he could start the day over.

"Okay, and what about the other hostages?" Smith continues.

Jeremy glances over at the family and then back at Rahab. He leans in to kiss her. She's frightened; he can tell.

"They're yours." He kisses Rahab tenderly, tasting her lips in spite of Puah's grunts. *This is my dream.*

"Oh, hells no!" Puah declares. "Over my dead body." She stands, preparing to march over, but Mr. Jenkins grabs her arm and yanks her down with a force that catches her off guard.

"Sit down," he demands, glaring directly into her eyes. "You'll only make our situation worse."

"Let go of me, James," Puah mutters through curled lips.

"Yeah. I suggest you handle ya woman, Pops," Jeremy states, moving from the door. Rahab jumps in front of him, knowing he's easily irritated.

Puah grips the bridge of her nose and breathes out a *woosah*. "You know...just because your life is jacked up doesn't give you the right to drag ours through it." She is tired of quietly sitting by. It isn't her style.

"Shut up, Pu," Silas grunts. They all know once Puah gets started, it's hard to control her.

Jeremy bursts into maniacal laughter. He's had enough of Puah. "You just can't leave well enough alone, can you?" he directs toward her, waving his gun in the air.

"You ain't taking my child," Puah screams, pointing her erect finger and rolling her neck in attitude. "You chose your lifestyle; she didn't. If you REALLY love Rah, you'd let her go! You know you going to jail, right? YOUR major drug deal JUST got busted and that's not OUR problem." As soon as she said it, she knew she went too far, and it reads on her face. "and not Rah's fault…it's yours." Puah mumbles, turning her head.

Jeremy freezes. His mind recycles the information. *No one here knows…about the drug deal.* His mind wanders back. He's been mindful not to mention it. He turns to look at Rahab. *She's guilty.* Then, he remembers how strange she was acting the other night and how much information he released in anger. *She would never. She knows how much I hate small places…would she?* He looks at her again. She's flushed and doesn't have a poker face. *Damn it, Canaan was right, rest his soul. She got in the way of business.* What little heart Jeremy has left breaks and maniacal laughter turns into sobbing. "Noo, Rah!" he yells in a singing tone of voice as he dances around the room in anger and hurt pride, swinging the gun.

He suddenly grabs Rahab and pulls her into a hug. Life doesn't matter without her. *Why try to live?* Jeremy questions himself, thinking about the cops waiting to arrest him. "Why would you do this to us? You know I can't do jail."

I AM RAHAB

Keeping Rahab near is making the sniper's job complicated. They don't want to take him out, they just want him disarmed long enough to raid the apartment.

"I...I didn't do anything," Rahab attempts to convince Jeremy, but she's aware that *the jig is up*.

"Shut up," he shouts, spinning her around to face her family. With one arm wrapped around her neck, he places the gun on her temple. The family gasps and stands.

If it is possible to smell death, Rahab can. The foul-smelling odor passes through Jeremy's pores and ripples from his breath.

"Why, Rah? Why?" Jeremy continues to shout over her silent terror, but she doesn't answer him. There's nothing to say; her words can't undo what's already been said. Rahab's his captive, yet more than a prisoner.

Jeremy's mind screams for him to surrender, *raise the white flag*. But prison isn't an option. *Yo! Players don't go out like that. They go out HARD.* His sanity debates with the sense of insanity gripping him. Rahab's trembling body held against his alerts him, *it's not about the game anymore; she's involved*. He releases a sigh of despair.

"I love you," he reluctantly confesses; three words he's never uttered before, then plants a sloppy wet kiss on Rahab's forehead. "If this is it...it's gonna be you and me forever. *Bonnie* and *Clyde* style," he concludes, drawing her nearer as though trying to consume her. His trembling hand tightly grips the gun pressing against her temple.

Click. He cocks the pistol, ignoring the pleas from around the room. All he can hear is his own heavy breathing. *I always hated the way that movie ended.* He prefers to hold his and Rahab's destinies in his hands.

"Hi, Jeri," a tiny voice utters, yawning.

Charlotte walks into the living room humming a tune and rubbing her eyes. She wraps her arms around Jeremy's waist from behind. His body goes limp. Crying isn't his thing, but he can't seem to stop. His spirit is in mourning.

"Move, Cutie Pie," he softly urges, nudging her away from him. He'd forgotten Charlotte.

She had just awakened from a nap and was oblivious to what was happening. She and Krystal were told to lay down earlier because they were getting in the way of the movers.

"Come here, Cookie," Puah calmly requests as not to startle her. The rest of the family quietly gestures her over.

Charlotte ignores them and starts to softly sing to Jeremy's situation like his sister used to do. As though well planned, every word speaks directly to him. He crumbles inside, bulldozed by the beginning verses of *"Heal the World."*

"Did you bring me cake?" Charlotte asks, retreating from their hug.

Jeremy doesn't answer. She's annihilated him. His only conclusion is to feel what she feels. He wants to be in that special place she's managed to master.

At that moment, as others have said before, time seems to stand still. The family, helplessly watching the ordeal freezes. Their faces grimace in agony. Rahab's own tears stop flowing and plaster her face. She can't move. Her body becomes stiff. From the corner of her eyes, she looks up at Jeremy. His eyes, frozen upon her, have lost their intensity. He doesn't look like himself. He seems conflicted. A war between good and evil plays upon his face. Rahab's body numbs. A calming peace washes over her. She closes her eyes and gives everything she has to Him.

BANG! A gun fires.

Rahab can see *Big Mama* boiling sheets. Herself, young and innocent, underfoot. She can feel the warmth of the hot steam coming up from the boiling pot.

Am I dead? Her life vividly flashes before her.

She and Jeremy both fall into Charlotte's arms. Charlotte attempts to carry their weight but the pressure forces her to release them. It appeared they both took the bullet. Jeremy never released Rahab from the headlock and brings her down on top of him.

Shocked, Rahab lays motionless on Jeremy's chest. His warm blood soaks the back of her sweater. Charlotte kneels over them, maybe not as oblivious as everyone thinks. She closes Jeremy's eyes. Slowly, the rest of the family migrates toward them. Their mouths are moving but Rahab's ears are ringing, and she can't hear. The room is still and sad. Scared and tense. Consumed and empty. At Charlotte's touch, Rahab slowly turns her head.

"Am I dead?" she asks loudly, unable to hear herself speak. She frantically frisks her body.

Charlotte shakes her head *no*. Rahab closes her eyes and sighs in relief, then thinks of Jeremy. *He isn't moving;* his arm is loose around her neck. Tears instantly puddle her eyes. A piercing scream fills the pit of her stomach, building in momentum before launching from her mouth and popping her ears.

"Jeri? Jeri!"

JC MILLER

BY FAITH

Steaming hot white linen hangs drenching wet above her head. The fragrance of Big Mama's signature scent of rosemary and lavender oil drift through the dense swampy air. The chanting song of the cicadas accompanied by the throaty hymn of the bullfrog compete with the rolling of boiling water. Rahab wonders, positioning herself between dripping sheets and allowing their shade to shield her from the blazing Louisiana sun. *Why do you love me so?* She inquires of the Lord as Salmone passes her clothespins. Her golden sand-colored hair blows against a subtle breeze, and she stops working to tame her locks. Taking notice of her beauty and her hands busy with work, Salmone hangs his clothespin bag on the line and embraces her. She playfully squirms and frees her mouth of gathered clothespins.

"Come on now, quit. We'll be here all day if we keep at it like this."

Salmone constantly gifts her with acts of affection. Rahab makes him proud, and every day in his arms is a blessing to her. His love is fulfilling. It inflates her heart beyond levels she hadn't realized it could reach. Acts of intimacy no longer usher tears of sorrow, only those of joy.

Salmone bends and nuzzles the crease of her sweaty neck.

"Poo-yie!" he jokingly expresses, squeezing her tighter.

They laugh. Rahab tilts her head as he releases an overflow of kisses on her neck and shoulders. She's everything he hoped for and more than he could ever imaginc.

I AM RAHAB

"Our worlds may not blend with a love song, and most likely they don't match the beauty the Lord has playing against them, but I love you, and our love makes its own music," Salmone states, rendering his love language that he keeps on repeat.

Rahab looks up at him. The sun behind his head projects a halo. She squints and encloses his face with her hands, pulling him down into a kiss. Even their lips match.

"How perfect are you?" she asks, considering their world a dream sometimes.

"Perfectly made for you," he answers, tucking stray hairs behind her ear.

"Let's go fishing," she states spontaneously. The laundry can wait but our love cannot. She's learned that time is neither friend nor foe; it just ticks.

"Now you're talking my language," Salmone shouts, tapping her on her derriere.

"Mmm, let's not turn this into something else," Rahab warns, winking. He's as fine as the days are long.

"You ain't said nuttin' but a thang," Salmone growls and stomps his foot like a bull readying to charge.

Rahab knows he's kidding, but the realistic sound always sends her screaming and running. She circles the clothesline and hides behind a sheet. He finds her and growls as she screams and runs for a shed.

Over their laughter, the faint cry of a toddler is heard. Rahab sighs and places her tackle box back on the shelf.

"We tried," Salmone relates, knowing she seeks to please him.

"Baby's up!" Mags yells from the kitchen window of their gray and black farmhouse. She notices the young couple have their minds set on fishing. "Y'all go on. Me and this one here are going to have us some lunch."

"Thanks, Tante Maw-Maw. I'll bring you back a good dinner," Salmone declares, pulling his wife along before she changes her mind.

Mags laughs, "Make sure that's all you bring back. I ain't taking care of any more of these little critters," she jokes, lifting Boaz from his playpen and kissing his chubby cheeks. "Grand T-Maw is getting old, ain't it sugha."

***

Rahab's life has come full circle. Her birth has met her coming of age. It's been an arduous trip, a jolting rotation, but she's discovered purpose along the way. What she lost in the city, she's found in the bayou. The voice of maturity notes, *life is just beginning.*

The bayou welcomed her back home. The cypress trees bowed upon her arrival and caped her shoulders in Spanish moss. The starry nights crown her head and the earth embraces her with fields of lavender, as spacious as her name. With her gifted hands, she cultivates and manufactures a beauty line called *Lotti*. No Voodoo required.

Often, the thing you need the most is right under your nose. Unfortunately, it sometimes takes a journey to find. Rahab can't say that her journey has been disappointing thus far, she's blossoming and leaving seedlings along the way. Every day isn't perfect but each day she's perfect in Christ Jesus, *fearfully and wonderfully made.* She misses her family but not as much as she thought she would. Her existence no longer relies on their coexistence. The separation made their love stronger, and now reunions are a time for celebration, reflection, and rediscovery.

The family is getting along well. Silas quit his job at the loading dock. Now he co-leads a street ministry with Pastor Paul called T.E.N.T.S (Too Empowered Not To Shine). They set up awareness programs throughout the city geared toward recovery, education, re-establishment, support, and recompense. He also accepted the opportunity to minister as lead pastor to a growing congregation on Charlotte Street. The South Bronx welcomed Silas home. His messages come from a familiar place and lead to a loving Father. His youth is no hindrance; the Word is in his heart. He and Lydia, along with their children, Krystal and Christian, live in a modest home in Yonkers. The house is cozy enough for four yet large enough for three more. Puah, Mr. Jenkins, and Charlotte also reside in the five-bedroom, two and a half bath Victorian. They no longer depend on the streets; they *lift up their eyes to the hills.*

Puah finally put her tarot cards aside. Silas' sermons whispered in secret places and before long, her cards read *washed in the blood* of Jesus. She, Mr. Jenkins, and Charlotte were baptized together.

Lydia is still changing lives hosting bible studies for strippers and prostitutes. Her clientele places her and her team in high regard. Her small, successful storefront made way to a warehouse. *Purple Palace* is the official *Danskin* to divas. Her costumes adorn the people God placed in her heart to serve. Her motto, *"Dress the body, touch the soul"* comes from her humble start dressing Rahab in remnants, second-hand finds, and love.

Nine months after moving back home, Gomer had another son. She struggled for a while but finally put her wings into flight. Always having a flair for hair, she worked for Lydia while attending cosmetology school. She now owns a day spa featuring her sister's beauty products.

God's thoughts are not our thoughts. His ways are not our ways. He heals the broken in heart and binds up their wounds. He takes what we consider as broken pieces and fits them together in brilliant harmonies. He is our Father; He is the potter and we are the clay. We all are the work of His hand.

The spiritual slate is wiped clean for those who believe. It doesn't change *who you are*, but rather *how you are*. Your perception is altered as though putting on *God glasses* and filtering life through *His lenses*.

Therefore if anyone is in Christ, he is a new creation. The old things have passed away. Behold, all things have become new. 2 Corinthians 5:17

EPILOGUE - THE BIBLICAL STORY OF RAHAB

Rahab the Harlot, one of the most thought-provoking and compelling heroines of the Old Testament, lived in the *Promised Land* of *Jericho*. She was a woman of faith whose actions spoke of her belief.

It is notably clear that *Rahab* was insightful, witty, and loyal. The city of Jericho where she dwelt was part of a pagan culture as well as a city under God's condemnation. Living inside of the legendary wall of Jericho acquainted Rahab with the in's and out's of the fortress. Having her finger on the city's pulse, she immediately recognized the Israelite spies for who they were and, against any indication of danger, hid them on her roof. Her faith in their God, whom she had only heard of, was more significant than the fear of her conditions.

Rahab lied to questioning officials when they came to her looking for the men. She placed herself in imminent danger saying, *"...where the men went, I don't know. Pursue them quickly; for you will overtake them."*

Once the spies were safe, she begged them for their protection. When an oath was made, she gave them sound advice, telling them to hide in the mountains for three days before going their way. She then *let them down by a rope through the window*.

Rahab was an exemplary woman of faith! She enters the Bible as a harlot and becomes one of the leading ladies on Jesus' family tree. A harlot is an ancestor of *the Messiah*! Matthew 1:1-16 outlines the genealogy starting with father *Abraham to Joseph, the husband of Mary, from whom was born Jesus, who is called Christ;* with *Salmon, Rahab, and Boaz* falling amongst the account. Royalty! One day a prostitute, the next living amongst chosen people. Who does that but God?

But Joshua spared Rahab the prostitute, with her family and all who belonged to her, because she hid the men Joshua had sent as spies to Jericho—and she lives among the Israelites to this day." - Joshua 6:25

Rahab was grafted into the lineage of Christ because of her faith. The Bible says that as believers we are also assigned an inheritance in him, having been foreordained according to the purpose of him who does all things after the counsel of his will (Ephesians 1:11). What that means is that as children of God we are to expect an inheritance. Secondly, we gain eternity with the Lord.

In the existence of Rahab, we discover the inspiring story of all *wildflowers* plucked by unmerited favor. We don't share the same journeys, being individually pressed against our own realities, but we share in the common need of a loving savior. Rahab is you and I. We're beautiful flowers growing wild against this green-screen called life.

According to the Midrash, which is an ancient commentary, our girl Rahab is named one of the four most beautiful women the world has ever known. She shares her billboard with Sarah, Abigail, and Esther. God gave Rahab a garland for her ashes, oil of joy for her mourning, and the garment of praise for the spirit of heaviness.

Wildflowers, attention! The Wall of *Jericho* is before us but be of good cheer for *the battle is not ours. Be strong in the Lord, and in the strength of his might.* Know that God loves you and His greatest desire is for you to come into a relationship with Him through Jesus Christ. The rest of *His plan* for *your life* will unfold as you live and learn. I

encourage you to read the Bible, enter into an intimate relationship with Him through prayer, live an obedient life, fellowship with other believers and share His love.
    The End

CHARACTER GLOSSARY

Rahab	the Harlot	Joshua 2, Joshua 6, Matthew 1:5, Hebrews 11:31, James 2:25
Puah and Shiphrh	Midwives who attended the births of the Hebrew women. They were ordered by Pharaoh to kill the baby boys but let the girls live.	Exodus 1
Lydia	The first documented convert to Christianity in Europe. A seller of purple.	Acts 16
Joshua	Succeeded Moses as leader of the Israelites.	Exodus, Numbers, and Joshua
Gomer	Wife of the prophet Hosea. Referred as a *promiscuous woman*.	Hosea
Hosea	Prophet of doom	Hosea
Silas	Leading member of the early Christian church. Accompanied Paul on his missionary journeys.	Acts
Paul	An Apostle. First mentioned in Acts as Saul. Penned thirteen of the Epistles.	I and II Thessalonians, Titus, Galatians, Romans, I and II Corinthians,

I AM RAHAB

		Philippians, Philemon, Ephesians, I and II Timothy and Colossians.
Salmon	mentioned in both the Old Testament and in the New Testament. He was married Rahab, and Boaz was their son.	Believed to be one of the two spies sent to Jericho by Joshua. Matthew 1:5, 1 Chronicles 2:10-1, Ruth 4:20-21, Luke 3:32.
Boaz	Appears in the book of Ruth. His parents are named as Salmon and Rahab. Boaz was a wealthy landowner who notices and later marries the widow Ruth.	Both in the Old and New Testament. Ruth, Matthew 1:5, Luke 3:32 and 1 Chronicles 2:11-12
Mary Magdalene	Traveled with Jesus as one of his followers. Believed to be a repentant prostitute and also the same Mary who was freed of seven demons.	Gospel of Mark, Gospel of Matthew, Gospel of Luke, Gospel of John

JC MILLER

Auguste Family Tree

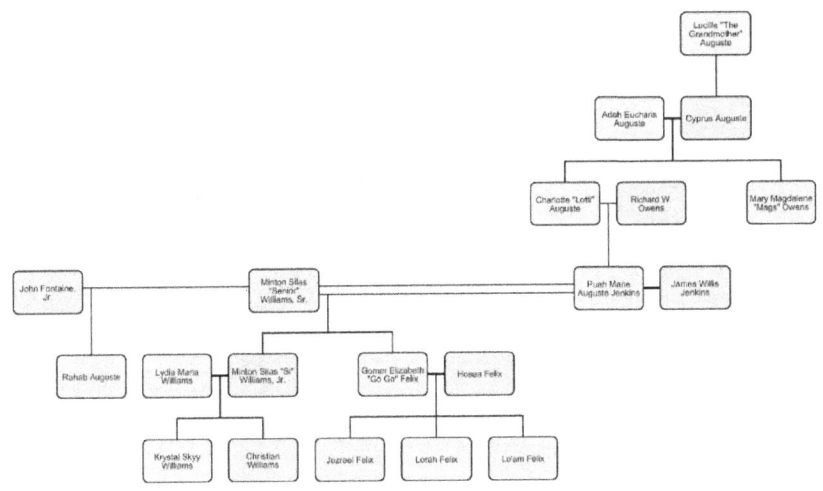

Stay tuned for the next induction of the I AM series - They Call Me Gomer, coming in 2020

Made in the USA
Middletown, DE
22 September 2020